Leah and the Final Whistle?

To Rosie

Best wishes,

Paul Mullins

Paul Mullins

Illustrated by Steve Brookes

Copyright 2016

Dedication

To Philippa Hanna and Joel Cana
To Milford Athletic Meteors
To Wyrley Juniors

Acknowledgements

The title to the opening book of this series, *Leah and the Football Dragons* was decided at the last minute when my brother-in-law discovered there was already a book published called *Girls Can't Play Football* and I didn't want to use a title that already existed.

When *Leah and the Waiting Game* was written, I knew I had put myself into a situation where this book needed a title in the same format.

The title of this one was debated over – did the word 'Final' make it sound like it was a spoiler for this being the last story I write about Leah? Or, was it a good word to use for people to ask 'What final?' – A cup final, the end of something… You'll have to read on to find out!

As ever, there are people to mention in this book, without whom I wouldn't be writing this.

To the regular list of friends who have proofread this story.

To Donna and daughter Lauren, who played a virtual penalty shootout with me on Facebook to help me with a section of the book, while Lauren went to school dressed as Leah for World Book Day.

To Shauna, whose daughter Evie also went as a footballer for World Book Day.

To Colin, who photoshopped the background photo for the cover.

To Keith and all at Wyrley Juniors, who presented all of their girls' teams with a signed copy of *Leah and the Football Dragons* for the Football Association initiative *Girls Football Week.*

And, of course, to you, who keep on coming back for more stories about Leah. Thank you.

Chapter 1

"Dad! I've found it!" Leah called from the living room, where she was sat with the local newspaper.

Jeff entered the room from the kitchen, holding a mug of hot tea and stood next to the sofa, overlooking his daughter.

"Found what?"

"The advert," Leah said, turning round the newspaper.

"Marshbrook Maidens," Jeff began, "are inviting applications for the position of first team manager. Following their successful season last year which resulted in promotion, manager Annabel Davies retired. This created an exciting opportunity to take the team forward. Interested applicants should email their CV to Miss A. Davies who will oversee the appointment of her successor."

"I wonder who will apply," Leah pondered.

Jeff shuffled into the kitchen out of Leah's earshot, where son Mikey was helping Rose drying up the dinner plates.

"Do you think I should?" Jeff asked.

"Apply you mean?" Rose replied.

"Yes."

"That's up to you. You've already gone through the list of all of the pros and cons the night Annabel retired. You've had long enough to think about it."

"Toss a coin!" Mikey said, remembering how it worked for Leah when she needed to decide which of the girls' teams she would play for.

"Not a bad idea!" Jeff said, ruffling Mikey's hair.

He continued. "The big negative is whether it's a good idea to be the manager of my daughter's team!"

"But it is something you've always wanted to do," Rose stated. "You've said you've got the time to do it, and it's never bothered you that the job would be unpaid."

"Ever since I was a lad, I had always imagined myself being a manager or a coach…"

"But…"

"But, I just don't think it's fair on Leah to be her manager."

"Don't do it then. Wait for another team to come up, a boys' team so it won't affect Leah's career."

"Do it!" shrieked Mikey.

"I might just express an interest in case they don't find anyone. Annabel's been manager so long it'll be tough boots to fill!"

Jeff sneaked up the stairs while Leah was watching television, retreated to the office, powered up the laptop and tapped out a quick email to Annabel, stating that, "I have reservations about applying, but if you do not find a suitable candidate then please contact me and we will see whether it would work."

The closing date came and went and a few days afterwards, there was an update on the club's Twitter account to state that Annabel's replacement will be announced at the end of the week. Annabel texted the girls to advise them to report to training on Thursday to meet the new manager before it's announced officially.

Leah's phone was pinging with text after text from her teammates as to who it might be, whether any of them had an inkling or had heard a rumour.

Of course, there was always one girl who was convinced she knew for certain who it was. Zara Perry had stated with 100% certainty that she had already been told who the new manager was and that they had been appointed **before** Annabel had said she was retiring!

This was all because her Dad had bought Marshbrook's kit for several seasons and was very important to the club (according to Zara) for contributing a few hundred pounds worth of sponsorship.

When all the girls asked Zara who it was, she suddenly was "very busy at the moment" and wouldn't say!

At 7.30pm sharp on a warm summer's evening, fifteen of the Marshbrook Maidens players congregated outside the changing rooms and waited for someone to turn up.

Some of the parents had waited with the girls, including Jeff, but, by now he obviously already knew he hadn't been required to take up the job.

Eventually, at a little before quarter to eight, Annabel's car pulled into the car park and she slowly got out of the car to walk over to the Maidens.

There were a few aghast faces.

Annabel sensed this, "No, no, no!" she said. "It's not me taking over again, come into the changing room and your new manager will be here any moment to introduce herself."

The girls occupied the benches, forming a semi-circle around Annabel. By now, the mums and dads had headed off home which meant that none of those were the new manager either! Zara knew it wasn't her Dad too. A few of the girls had looked at Zara as her Dad drove off, as if to say, "You were saying?"

Annabel began to speak.

"Okay ladies. Since we got promoted…"

The girls cheered at that, interrupting Annabel in full flow.

"Since we got promoted…" she continued, "believe it or not it was harder finding someone to manage us than if we had stayed in the division we were in last year."

There were a few disappointed faces among the squad.

"We had a few applicants who were willing to help out…" Annabel said, turning to Leah and then to Zara, "yours included."

There was a murmur of joy that Zara's Dad hadn't been given the job to manage them and they suspected that Zara had assumed her Dad would get it looking at her crestfallen face.

"And," Annabel resumed, "we had a few people apply who would have been very good managers but weren't that keen when we pointed out that they wouldn't be getting paid in the job!"

There was a gentle knock at the changing room door.

"Two seconds!" Annabel demanded. "Let me introduce you first!"

The girls listened to hear if the mysterious door knocker spoke even a brief, "Okay" but there was silence.

"One person stood out from those who applied. Someone who reminded me of me when I was a young manager."

There were a couple of giggles among the girls. They couldn't imagine someone as old as Annabel was ever young!

Annabel continued, "She is vibrant, positive, encouraging and someone you will have come across before."

This got a few of the girls looking at each other with puzzled expressions.

"Someone who impressed me so much last season when I least expected it..."

The fifteen girls' faces were baffled, even Zara, who clearly didn't know who it was going to be whatever she might have claimed.

"Please welcome your new manager..."

The door opened.

"Wow!"

"Yes!"

"Wicked!"

"Who is it?" rang around the changing room.

Only one player, Leah, said her name out loud the second the door opened and, without thinking, had run up to her to give her a huge hug.

The slim figure of Hannah Wagstaff walked into the changing room.

"Ladies, Miss Hannah Wagstaff," Annabel introduced.

Hannah began to speak. "Good evening, I am sure you remember me from the game last season... Sorry!" she said sheepishly.

"Yeah! I remember," Maddy Baker the goalkeeper groaned.

Hannah continued. "I was manager of Southsea Swallows last year, and, of course I know Leah very well from her time with us. Annabel stated after our shock victory over you that she was surprised I had the managerial skills to get a team like Southsea to beat a team as organised as yourselves."

Annabel nodded.

"So," Hannah continued her welcoming speech, "once Annabel had started to decide enough was enough as a manager, she had rung me and said she would keep a close eye on Southsea's results in the league."

"Then," Annabel interrupted, "when we won promotion and I called it a day on my career, there was, for me, only one manager young enough and vibrant enough to take this club into the next division and keep us there for a few years at least."

"I hope I'll get us promoted again!" Hannah interjected.

"Welcome!" Annabel said proudly, shaking Hannah by the hand to seal the deal officially.

"Welcome Hannah!" said pretty much all of the players in unison. Zara didn't say anything, but no-one was surprised by that!

"Get yourselves changed girls and we'll do a short training session tonight, a bit of five-a-side football, basic skills sets but we'll finish up earlier than normal so if you want to have a chat with me then the door is open for you to do so," Hannah said, cheerily.

Hannah looked around the semi-circle of girls.

While the girls started to get changed, Hannah talked more loudly above the hubbub of the changing room.

"Like most new managers at clubs, there are players here that probably won't want to play under my leadership, so if you do want to look for another club, I will support you fully and you would leave with my blessing," she added.

Hannah and Annabel departed from the changing room to allow the girls to get ready for the first pre-season training session, knowing that there would be one or two of them that would want to speak to their teammates away from the new manager.

Annabel whispered, barely audibly as they left, "I am sure I made the right choice Hannah!"

For simplicity and quickness, Hannah divided the girls into teams and threw an orange football into the centre circle and watched studiously as the mini-match took place before her.

While the girls had a brief kickabout, with gleeful enthusiasm, Hannah watched on and one by one called each girl over during the match and chatted to them whether they wanted to continue playing at Marshbrook.

By the time half an hour had passed, Hannah had the phone numbers, email addresses and Facebook names of each of them and all the players from the previous season had agreed to remain a Marshbrook Maiden.

Even Zara was impressed that her new manager would be better than if her Dad had got the job, while Leah (and Jeff when he talked about it later that evening) were quite relieved that he hadn't got the job either!

It was clear that Leah had a new lease of life after the previous season had ended and was making passes to teammates and scoring goals that had every single girl applauding.

The following training session was very similar to the first, Leah was showing all the signs of maturing into a better player this season than she had ever been before.

It hadn't gone unnoticed with Daisy Ferguson, Charlotte Thornton and Niamh Oliver either. The three of them huddled together and whispered to one another that one of them was in danger of losing their place in the team to Leah.

In fact, over the next three weeks, they had been texting one another after school saying it was certain that Leah would be in the team in place of one of them, particularly as Daisy wrote, "Leah is Hannah's favourite from before!"

Aside from the discussions about Leah the golden one, the training was very enjoyable. Hannah was younger than Annabel, fitter than Annabel and was far more enthusiastic than their previous manager had been.

There was an infectiousness about her that made you want to run two miles when she asked you to run one, made you want to do forty press ups when she asked for twenty.

Hannah firmly believed that a happy football team would be a successful one.

At times, the girls didn't feel like they were working hard at all, but in the late summer months their training tops and football shirts were dripping with sweat by the end of each hour-long session.

Hannah gathered all the girls together into a circular huddle and spoke out, "I have a really good feeling about this season!"

Chapter 2

Just like the six weeks' school holidays, the length of time between the last game of the previous season and the first game of the new one came around increasingly quickly.

The first game of the season was at home against Littleborough. They had been relegated from division six a year ago, whereas Marshbrook had been promoted from division eight. So, on paper at least, a year ago the two sides had been two leagues apart.

Hannah didn't have a clue what to expect from her opponent. Their record last year had been: played eighteen, lost eighteen, scoring only five goals and conceding over one hundred!

"That means nothing!" Hannah declared in her first official team talk as manager of Marshbrook.

"It means they are rubbish!" one of the girls whispered. Hannah didn't know who.

"Nope!" Hannah stated abruptly. "It means last year they were the weakest team in their league. That's all! There's no room for complacency. They could have eleven new players. They **were** two leagues higher than us!"

Some of the girls agreed. Some looked blankly. At least Hannah knew there was a chance that the whisperer was one of the girls that gave her a blank look.

Hannah slowly read out her first team selection and the girls were gasping at the omission of Leah's name in the starting eleven.

As one they turned towards Leah and then looked towards Hannah!

"Boss?" Zara piped up.

"Yup."

"Erm… Leah was our best player in pre-season, probably the best we've got here."

"Yup," Hannah replied, "but, if I had an office and an office door," she chuckled nervously, "it would be my name on it and the word **Manager** underneath. I pick the team. Get changed."

It was the most stern the Marshbrook girls had ever seen Hannah. There was no cheery smile, no chirpiness in her voice.

Leah had seen her like this before, the time that Hannah had been wound up by a newspaper article about Annabel Davies and Marshbrook Maidens concerning how many goals they would beat Southsea Swallows by. Hannah had been angered and determined and clinical that day. She was the same now.

Leah didn't say much. Her teammates' reaction had said it all.

With a confident murmur or two about how Marshbrook were going to "kick some bums!" and "thrash Littleborough" the girls got changed quickly and reached over to the neatly folded football shirts in the middle of the changing room and put on the appropriate number.

Leah took a gulp as she picked up her shirt. She thought it was impossible that she wouldn't be wearing the number nine shirt today. That was made worse as the number twelve shirt that she would be wearing was slightly overlapped by the number nine shirt which she had to touch to move out of the way.

Tilly Adams was still captain after last year and, when all the girls were ready, she lined up first, followed by goalkeeper Maddy Baker and the other nine starters with Leah bringing up the rear in a sweater top over her kit to keep warm.

There was a knock on the changing room door from the assistant referee and a hullabaloo of "Come on Maidens!" and hand clapping before the players exited the changing rooms and down towards the pitch.

Hannah fist-pumped each player as they walked past. All, but Leah. She put her arm across her to stop her proceeding and said, "Just a quiet word Lee."

"Boss...?"

Hannah replied, "There's no need for boss!"

"Sorry!"

"I heard a few things in training from the girls saying that as I had been your manager before that you would be the 'golden child' of the team and always get picked!"

"Oh... I hadn't... heard..." Leah mumbled.

"I should have spoken to you before. I'm sorry. I wanted to prove a point today that no-one has a divine right to start a game. I know you played well all summer."

Leah looked away from Hannah briefly to avoid eye contact.

"You were the best by far. I just... er... made a decision which will either be right or wrong by the time the whistle blows for full-time."

Leah wasn't sure whether to be angry at the decision or be grateful that Hannah was, at least, honest with her. So, Leah said all she could say in that situation, looking her manager in the eye with a simple, "Okay."

Hannah probably hadn't anticipated which way Leah would react as Leah walked out onto the pitch and Hannah walked slowly behind.

As Hannah locked the changing room doors, she pondered whether it was an "Okay, I understand," "Okay, thank you for telling me, but it's not fair," or "Okay, I have nothing to say so I better say something."

Hannah hated texts that said just "Okay" – saying it face-to-face was just as bad.

If Marshbrook had been complacent about winning, they got an early shock. Straight from the kick off, a quite bulky centre forward for Littleborough chased down a Marshbrook defender after the ball had been passed backwards to her.

Abby panicked at the sheer size of the girl approaching her. She attempted to clear the ball hurriedly and smashed it against the stomach of the Littleborough player. The ball fell to the girl's feet and she calmly pushed the ball forward and launched it past a bemused Maddy for a 1-0 lead.

Hannah looked sheepishly towards Leah as if to say "Oops!" but Leah was already on her feet, clapping her hands rapidly and shouting, "Remember our training! Concentrate! We'll win this!"

Hannah looked approvingly at Leah, whispered "Captain material" under her breath and shouted some instructions towards the stunned Maidens.

It didn't take long for Marshbrook to equalise the scores though with Niamh Oliver grabbing the first goal of the season, before Abby redeemed herself for the error by heading home Niamh's corner kick for a half-time lead of 2-1.

A goal for Charlotte Thornton and another goal for Abby quickly made it 4-1 at the start of the second half and Littleborough's players looked demoralised – a feeling they knew so well from the previous season.

Leah was warming up vigorously on the touchline as if to say "Come on boss!" and Hannah saw the errors of her ways from the start of the game and introduced Leah as substitute.

Niamh got her second goal, quickly followed by a hat-trick goal for Abby before Marshbrook rounded off an 8-1 win with another goal from striker Charlotte Thornton and one from Eloise Milns.

Leah didn't get a goal but took great satisfaction from setting up three of the four goals that were scored while she was on the field.

Eloise was beaming from ear to ear at scoring only the second goal of her career, a goal of astonishing individual skill for a defender during which she twisted and turned past six defenders before cheekily rolling the ball through the legs of the Littleborough keeper.

"Great goal Messi!" the girls said one by one as they patted her on the back as she left the pitch.

She loved her nickname. Lionel Messi had been her idol ever since they had done anagrams at primary school and the teacher had noted that Eloise Milns was an anagram of the Argentina and Barcelona player!

Back in the changing room, Hannah praised the girls with a simple, "Job done! See you at training on Thursday!" and the girls showered and got changed back into their day-to-day clothes before making their way home.

Leah was a little disillusioned at training. She felt that if her best ever form in pre-season wasn't going to be enough to get in the team, what did she have to do?

Even though Hannah had explained her reasons, Leah **didn't** feel it was very fair and decided to show Hannah how wrong she was!

When the training session was over and all the Maidens made their way back to get changed and go home, Leah took her shin pads out from her socks, placed them neatly by her bag and went for a run around the pitch.

During the first lap, Hannah hadn't noticed Leah hadn't gone to get changed. So, Leah did a second lap, running as fast as she could on the far side of the pitch and slowing down when she got near to Hannah to ensure her boss saw her!

She still didn't. Hannah went off to the changing room while Leah did a third lap out of stubbornness – the fastest of the three.

By the time Leah re-joined the other girls in the changing room, they were already changed and Leah looked a very tired figure as she threw her bag down onto the benches.

"You don't have to prove anything!" Hannah called from the other side of the room, just out of sight around a corner.

"Huh?"

"I told you I made a mistake in the first game and that I should have picked you. You don't have to prove to me that I was wrong. I already know."

"I did it for me!" Leah lied. "Annabel used to say I got a bit fat over the summer."

"Hmm," Hannah mumbled. "Get changed Leah, your Dad's already here waiting for you."

Chapter 3

After an impressive opening day victory, game two was an away trip to Castleton. Leah had done some research and seen that they had finished fourth last season, missing out on promotion by just one point. They had drawn their opening game of the season with the team that had finished fifth last season.

After having to apologise to Leah for leaving her on the substitutes' bench in the first game, Hannah had to apologise again to say that it would be unfair to change the line-up from the side that had won so comprehensively.

Leah had come to expect it this time. She knew enough about football to know that very few managers change any of the players when they have just won.

She knew Hannah believed in her ability and knew in this new league, there would be games that were tougher than their game with Littleborough and she knew she'd get her chance. This time she was ready to play the waiting game!

Castleton had the most garish kit Leah had ever seen! The main body of the shirt was plain white. But, it had five horizontal stripes of decreasing thickness from top to bottom, starting with a thick pink stripe, followed by red, blue, yellow and orange, while all the stripes had fluorescent green dots randomly placed over the shirt as if someone had decided to flick paint with a paintbrush all over it!

The home side took an early lead which was quickly levelled out by Charlotte 'Thorny' Thornton's clever free kick that totally bamboozled the Castleton goalkeeper who had thought that the ball was going well wide of the post until it swerved rapidly and nestled in the corner of the net.

Castleton regained their advantage midway through the second half, forcing Hannah to replace a defender with the attacking nature of Leah, with Abby the player sacrificed for the Maidens.

No sooner had Leah crossed the white line onto the pitch, than 'Thorny' curled a pass over the defensive line of Castleton and Leah raced forward, side-footing the ball with her very first touch beyond the home goalkeeper.

Hannah leapt in the air to celebrate and then quickly resumed her poise and held up three fingers in a triangle formation to transmit a message that she wanted Charlotte and Niamh to drop back a bit towards the midfield and try and hold on to the draw they had seemed to have gained.

The Castleton manager was shouting a few yards away from Hannah, reminding his team how they had missed out on promotion by the smallest of margins last year and couldn't afford to waste opportunities to beat "poor opposition like these!"

He frantically waved his arms to encourage his girls into an attacking formation and forced Marshbrook back so far they were effectively playing with ten defenders and a goalkeeper.

Into the final seconds, Castleton's manager was having kittens! His face ever reddening with frustration that the ball wouldn't go into the goal. His team had hit the post three times, the crossbar once, slammed the ball against the bums, chests, backs and legs of the Marshbrook defenders but were unable to find the killer winning goal.

He looked at his watch. There couldn't have been more than thirty seconds remaining as the goalkeeper hit a high pass into the Marshbrook penalty area. The ball seemed to take an age to come down, eventually spinning onto the lower arm of Eloise.

"Penalty!" screamed the players.

"Handball!" shouted the manager.

The referee shook her head and said, "No penalty!" instead awarding a corner kick for Castleton. The tiny figure of the Castleton number 7 swung the ball towards the goal but Maddy Baker was confident and leapt high to pluck it out of the air.

The Castleton girls again moaned at the referee, surrounding her to complain again that the penalty wasn't given, forgetting that the game was still in progress!

Thinking quickly, Maddy scissor kicked the ball out of her hands into the path of Leah who was standing in acres of space while the garish girls were still congregated around the referee.

Leah couldn't believe her luck! No-one was anywhere near her. All she had to do was keep running with the ball and outfox the goalkeeper.

Leah was too quick for any of the home side to catch her up so the lanky goalkeeper was the only barrier between Leah and a late winning goal.

Having watched most of the game from the side lines, Leah remembered how Thorny's goal had tricked the keeper and swung her right boot towards the ball. Leah curled the ball using the outstep of the boot to the goalkeeper's right. And, just as she had failed to keep out the free kick, she couldn't get down low enough to parry the ball and Leah had won the game for Marshbrook!

The Castleton manager was kicking water bottles and chairs in the technical area of his dugout while Hannah had sprinted down the touchline to jump on top of the girls who were celebrating the goal. Even Maddy had run the full length of the pitch from her goal to pile on top of her teammates!

Two wins out of two quickly became three wins out of three with a tight 2-1 victory over Eastwell. Eloise and Zara had scored the Marshbrook goals before a frantic last few minutes saw Eastwell score a goal and then hit the crossbar twice to be denied a late equaliser.

The games came thick and fast and in the glorious sunshine at a team called Farthinghoe, Marshbrook scraped a narrow 1-0 win with a goal in the final minute from defender Sarah Kemp.

That made it a statistic of played four and won four. Only one other team in the league so far had also won all of their games and that was Nailsworth, who had not conceded a goal yet in their matches to date – and they were Marshbrook's next opponents.

Hannah concocted the most intense training session so far, swapping all of the players from their regular positions into unfamiliar ones. Defenders became midfielders, midfielders became strikers, and strikers became defenders.

By the time the late-September sun had set, the Maidens were dripping with sweat from head to toe and there wasn't one player who hadn't gone red in the face!

Nailsworth were the largest girls' team Leah had ever seen. She imagined that if she had kept in touch with some of the lads from Deadtail Dragons that this was how bulky they had grown into.

The shortest Nailsworth player was taller than the tallest Marshbrook player and the Maidens could see why they had over-powered all of their opponents so far this season.

After being left out of the first few games of the season, Leah had forced her way back into the team in place of Daisy Ferguson and had even earned the captain's armband off Tilly Adams.

Nailsworth bullied their way to an early 2-0 lead but when Zara became the first player to score a goal against them this season the 'Nailers' as they were unsurprisingly nicknamed suddenly seemed demoralised.

When Charlotte Black got her first goal this year to level the score at 2-2, Maidens were confident they could extend their winning start.

Nailsworth had other ideas and regained the lead at 3-2 before Maidens found some spirit from somewhere to bring the game level again at 3-3 with Thorny scoring a fluky goal following a corner kick, after the ball bounced off the referee straight into her path!

The Nailers surrounded the referee in fury, despite anyone with any sense knowing it was a pure accident. But, it was the Nailers who completely suffered head loss from that point and chance after chance fell to the Maidens until the breakthrough and winning goal finally came from the left foot of an in-form Eloise.

So, for the first time, Marshbrook were ahead of everyone and top of the league. On mobile phones and computers throughout the team and their families, screenshots and print screens were being made of the league table that proudly showed Marshbrook Maidens as number 1.

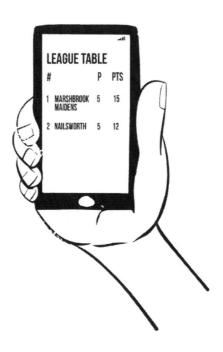

Hannah was getting so carried away with the excitement that she said to the players after the Nailsworth game, "The Swallows are flying!" to severe looks from the Maidens who reminded her she wasn't manager of Southsea Swallows anymore!

By way of an apology, and as a reward for being top of the league, Hannah said that after the next training session she'd meet them at KFC and they would celebrate.

Leah lay on her bed, again looking at the league table on her phone!

Although she was a teenager, she still had teddy bears and picked up one she'd had since she was four or five.

"Snowy," she whispered, cuddling him closely. "It looks like things are finally coming together for me! I'm in the team, we're doing well and life is good. We have still got a lot to look forward to this season!"

She glanced over at a noticeboard on her bedroom wall. Although it was still two months away, pinned there was a letter inviting her to Wembley Stadium for a keepy-uppy challenge.

Next to that was a photo of her boyfriend Luke.

She smiled.

Chapter 4

"This is almost too good to be true!" Leah stated, showing her Dad the league table on her phone, as if he didn't already know they were first.

Jeff had always tried to be positive about Leah's career but he also had enough knowledge of the game of football to know that good runs don't go on forever; that seasons can change in the blink of an eye.

It was something he had tried to drum into Leah, particularly during the season she struggled to get into the Marshbrook team and flew that nest briefly to be with Southsea.

But, right now, things were going well. Hannah had a formula at Marshbrook that suited the players she had – it was a classic 'Christmas Tree' formation, four defenders Abby, Sarah, Tilly and Eloise, three in front of them, Charlotte Black, Natasha and Zara, two in front of them, Charlotte Thornton and Niamh, with Leah at the top of the tree.

In fact, Leah now had a new nickname! Gone was the 'Boy Wonder' tag from her Deadtail Dragons days and now, in Hannah Wagstaff's Christmas tree, Leah was at the top of the formation, the 'Angel' on the tree.

Hannah's angel was certainly better than the taunting of Hannah's golden child at the start of the season!

The five win run eventually came to an end with an away trip to Wellington who kept the game tight, took control of possession and defended as if their lives depended on it to keep Marshbrook to a 0-0 draw.

Tilly found the game frustrating and lost her temper, shoving over a Wellington player as they left the field at full-time. The referee awarded her a red card and told Hannah that she would report it to the league, even though the game had finished.

After dropping points for the first time, Marshbrook had a break from league action with a trip down to Upton Cross in the Cup, laughing on the way at a road sign for a town called Minions just over a mile away.

So when Upton Cross walked onto the pitch with yellow shirts and blue shorts, the Marshbrook girls couldn't help but titter that the Upton players were actually Minions!

The girls had sent various tweets to say, "We are playing Minions" and Tilly, who hadn't travelled to the game due to her suspension, replied to say, "Keep saying 'Banana' in their ears as the game goes on!"

The referee blew the whistle to get the game under way and Upton Cross looked like they were ready to take the game on the attack and pin Marshbrook back into their own half.

Hannah made a few arm movements from the side line and Maidens held firm, keeping the score 0-0 throughout the first half and long into the second half.

As the time ticked on, Upton's players looked frustrated that they hadn't scored yet and Marshbrook grew in confidence that they could maybe go on an attack themselves to try and steal the game 1-0.

Alas, neither were to be and the full-time whistle from the referee seemed to come around as quickly as an exam at school that you forgot to revise for!

"Full-time!" hollered the referee, pointing to the centre circle and raising an arm upright, with her hand above her head. "Penalty shoot-out!" she continued.

Both sets of players gathered in tight circles, closely around their respective managers and there was a hubbub of activity among both teams.

Some girls looked away from their managers, others raised their arms like they were in the classroom at school, some pointed to their chests as if to say 'pick me' and others were chattily saying "Yeah, I'll take one" or "No way!"

Hannah submitted her list of all eleven names of her players in the order in which they would take the penalties if it went beyond the normal five kicks each.

The referee called over Leah and Upton's captain, tossed a coin and Upton called correctly and chose to go first.

Upton's number 7 stepped forward first and, to shouts of "Go on, Evie!" from her teammates, cheekily chipped the penalty down the middle. Maddy had already dived to her left and Upton gained an early advantage.

Leah took her captain's responsibility seriously and had proudly volunteered to be Marshbrook's first penalty taker.

She had no nerves, placed the ball on the white penalty spot and turned it round so that the logo on the ball faced her.

She took no more than four paces back and from a short run up, powered the ball confidently to the goalkeeper's left to score.

Upton scored their second kick, as did Niamh for Marshbrook and it was all square again at 3-3 and 4-4 with Abby and Sarah confidently scoring for the Maidens.

Upton's fifth kick, from a muddy girl whose number six you could barely see on the back of her shirt, sailed to Maddy's right, perfectly inside the post to give them a 5-4 lead and put all the pressure on Marshbrook's fifth kicker.

Eloise knew that if she missed this penalty kick that the game would already be lost. But, if she scored, the shoot-out would reach 'sudden death' with a round of kicks each until one team was the winner.

'Messi' placed the ball on the white penalty spot and stared at the Upton goalkeeper. She turned away and walked back to the edge of the penalty area, weighing up so many options in her head *High or Low? Left or right? Hard or soft?*

She had decided left and high, and as hard as she could kick it with her increasingly tired legs. She sprinted forward and just as she was about to kick the ball she remembered Upton's cheeky first penalty straight down the middle and changed her mind.

Eloise reached the ball and decided to kick the ball straight down the middle and hoped and prayed that the goalkeeper moved to one side or the other.

She didn't.

Whether or not the goalkeeper had a lucky guess of what Eloise might try we will never know. She just stood still, rigid in the middle of the goal and caught the ball as easily as if someone had thrown her a bag of sweets.

The Upton players sprinted towards their goalkeeper hero while Eloise was a lonely figure, her football jersey pulled over the head to hide the tears, as two players (she didn't know who) put their arms around her to console her.

The journey home was long and silent. A group of disappointed, demoralised players.

No-one blamed Eloise, of course. They all praised her for being one of the five courageous enough to volunteer.

But, Hannah's Christmas tree formation soon became akin to a house of cards collapsing back onto the table.

With defender Tilly Adams suspended from her sending off, Hannah then lost midfielder Natasha Holmes who tore a muscle at the back of her knee in a 4-1 defeat to Stony Hollow.

Then, Charlotte Thornton's grandad died suddenly and, as he had taught her to play football in the first place, she didn't want to play anymore.

Marshbrook's bad set of results continued, losing 3-2 to Morburn, although for Leah it wasn't a bad game, scoring two goals with her head – the first time she had ever done that in one game. Hannah barely had eleven players to choose from for the next game at home to Brightwood Belles and with Sarah Kemp picking up a nasty cut above her eye in the first ten minutes which needed a trip to A&E, Marshbrook were down to ten players for the whole game and suffered a humiliating 5-0 defeat.

At training, only eight players turned up, so when the Maidens arrived at their next away game at Eastwell, Hannah stood in the changing room like a teacher in a classroom and took a register of who had arrived!

"Maddy?"

"Here!"

"Good! At least we have a goalkeeper! Defenders…"

Abby, Eloise, Tegan and Tilly said, "Here!" in one go.

"Thank goodness your suspension is over Tilly!"

"Good to be back!" Tilly said, confidently.

"Charlotte, Natasha, Zara?"

"All here!" Zara said.

"Leah? Niamh? Daisy?"

"Here!" Leah and Niamh said in unison.

"Daisy?" asked Hannah again. "Don't we have anyone else?"

There was a deathly hush, quickly broken though by Daisy bustling into the changing room.

"Sorry I'm late!"

"Better late than never! Yay, we have eleven! Don't get injured girls!"

A shock early goal from Tegan Perkins gave Marshbrook a 1-0 lead and when Natasha made it 2-0, it seemed that the losing streak was coming to an end.

But, when Leah had a goal disallowed for offside, which everyone thought was the wrong decision, including the Eastwell players, Marshbrook seemed to have their enthusiasm zapped out of them.

Eastwell got one goal back at the start of the second half and then made the scores level with five minutes left. It was like Marshbrook had been stunned by a lightning bolt.

They then shrivelled up like flowers that hadn't seen sunlight for days and Eastwell, unsurprisingly, had the confidence to score again, to win 3-2.

Hannah and the girls slumped to the ground in despair. Back in the changing room there were tears.

Even when they were top, none of them had really thought that they were in an easy league. None of them had expected they would carry on winning. They didn't even mind if they lost if they had played well. It was because nothing seemed to be going right.

Injuries. Suspensions. Charlotte's grandad. What else could go wrong?

Hannah looked at her demoralised troops and stood up among them.

"That's it!" she said.

"What's it?"

"We can't go on like this. I have to do something."

"You're... not... quitting, are you?"

"Tempted! But, no. But this is the final straw, the final defeat for us. We need reinforcements!"

Chapter 5

"Dad! Help!" was all the text said.

Hannah knew that her Dad wasn't the most technologically savvy man she knew, so the shorter the message the better.

Harry didn't quite have an old brick phone but it didn't have the internet on it, so emails to him were out of the question. In fact, Hannah knew that she really should have rung him, rather than texting.

But, he knew how to read the text and immediately rang Hannah back.

"What's up?" he asked. "You could give a man an 'eart attack just putting 'elp like that!"

"We're on a losing streak Dad! I don't know if I can put it to an end!"

"You lost four in a row!" Harry replied. "'ow many did I lose in a row at Deadtail before Leah came along?"

"Too many to count!" Hannah chuckled.

"So, why you asking me for 'elp when I 'ad a worse record at Dragons?"

"Because..." she paused, "you know what you are doing, you know football... and... you're my Dad and I need you!"

"Okay, okay! Sold to the 'ighest bidder! You convinced me with that last one!"

"Thanks Dad, training is Thursday."

"Okay 'Annah! I'll be there."

It didn't take long for Harry to stamp his authority on the Marshbrook Maidens. It was like classic good cop, bad cop in all the movies. Hannah was the nice, positive, chatty one. Harry was the mean, argumentative, demanding one who got the girls to jump when he said so!

Such was the intensity of the training, the Maidens were finding muscles they didn't know existed and they were running around cones, stepping between the rungs of ladders lain on the floor and twisting and turning ways their bodies didn't know they could!

By the end of the first training session, there wasn't a girl who wasn't exhausted and breathing heavily – and that included the goalkeeper Maddy Baker who normally only had a few shots to save to improve her reflexes.

The proof of the pudding would be in the next match though and an early goal from Abby Moore gave Marshbrook a half-time lead and things looked a lot rosier all of a sudden.

But, perhaps Harry's training regime had been too intense. Natasha Holmes and Charlotte Black both suffered hamstring injuries and after using both substitutes to replace them, Hannah then lost Niamh Oliver to another hamstring injury and Marshbrook had to play on with ten players – again!

Barnstone Belles took full advantage of their opponent's disadvantages and scored two goals in a little over ten minutes to turn the game in their favour and then added two more goals to beat a beleaguered Marshbrook 4-1.

Despite playing much better, and even with five straight defeats Marshbrook got thinking that they **could** put this bad run to an end and faced a Castleton side at home in their next game, who themselves had lost four consecutive games.

Hannah and Harry thought the two teams would be evenly matched and for ten minutes they were right.

But, as a corner kick swung into the path of Maddy Baker, she was obstructed by a Castleton player just as she was about to catch the ball. Maddy fell to the floor, the ball fell to a Castleton striker and the visitors had a 1-0 lead.

The red mist descended on Maddy! Even though her teammates assured her that there was no foul and no deliberateness in the collision, Maddy had convinced herself there was.

She pushed her opponent with both of her gloved hands on the chest of the green jerseyed number nine who stumbled and fell backwards.

The referee saw everything and reached into his pocket for his cards, brandishing a red card in the face of Maddy!

Maddy trudged off towards the touchline, throwing her gloves to the floor as someone would need to replace her in goal. That task fell to poor Carrie Oakley, her first game back in the team this season.

(As Hannah looked around to see who to put in goal, every other player looked away and Carrie was the only one making eye contact with her manager.)

Maddy had to peel off her wet goalkeeping jersey, revealing an equally wet black T-shirt underneath and handed it to Carrie, who really didn't look pleased at having to wear it!

It soon became clear that Carrie wasn't a very good goalkeeper! Shot after shot flew past her. One. Two. Three. Four. Five by half-time. Six. Seven. Eight. Nine. Ten by full-time. A humiliating 11-0 defeat. At home!

The following training session was dominated by only one thing. With Maddy banned for the next two matches, they had to find someone who wanted to go in goal and was actually good enough!

This gave the girls a dilemma! None of them wanted to be in goal, but none of them wanted to let the team down either.

If they did well as goalkeeper, Hannah might keep them in goal for the next game, when they would rather be outfield trying to win the game for Marshbrook.

Harry and Hannah watched on studiously as Leah fired shots at all the potential goalkeepers. They had concluded that if they were to have any chance of winning their next game, they needed their best centre forward playing in her normal position, so there was no way they were going to use Leah as the goalkeeper.

Some of the girls were naturally too short to wear the number one jersey, and some were clearly uncoordinated and totally clueless when it came to saving the ball! They certainly didn't give Carrie another chance!

"'ere Boy Wonder!" Harry called, beckoning Leah over, calling her by her Deadtail Dragons nickname.

"Yes, boss number two?" as they called Harry.

"Remember when you got away with being a boy for us cos we were desperately bad and needed a decent player?"

"Y-e-s-s-s?" Leah said slowly, wondering what on earth Harry was going to suggest.

"Well, you know your boyfriend...?"

Leah looked puzzled. What did Luke have to do with any of this?

"Oh no, no, no, no! No, no, no, no, no!" Hannah butted in, guessing what her Dad was going to suggest.

"No what?" asked Leah.

"We are NOT, I repeat NOT getting Luke to pretend to be a girl so we have a great goalkeeper for the next match!"

"Boss?" Leah said, looking at Hannah. "You're not serious!?" she said, turning her attention to Harry.

"No way! No!" said Harry. "I was wondering, being as 'e is a good goalkeeper whether someone at 'is team knew of a gal that was really good and could sign for us for Sunday!"

Neither Leah nor Hannah knew whether Harry was serious with what he said.

"I can –," Leah said, interrupted before she could say the word 'ask'.

"It won't happen!" Hannah said. "We play Sunday! We have to register a new player by the end of tomorrow. Forget it Dad! Don't even ask him Leah. We will have to pick someone from who we have here!"

After half an hour of discussion over a coffee in the leisure centre café, defender Abby Moore was the 'lucky' one to be picked as goalkeeper in the upcoming game with Woodmead.

It didn't work out either! Marshbrook started well and took an early lead through Leah's first goal in a long time. But, once Abby had spilled an easy shot into her goal (that even Carrie said, "I would have saved that!") Woodmead got confident that they could score from anywhere!

Just like poor Carrie, the balls flew beyond Abby from every angle and in every corner as Woodmead rattled up an 8-1 lead. It was only when they used all three of their substitutes (Hannah wished she had that many she could use) and relaxed a bit that the Maidens got chance to score again. At least, Leah came out of the game with a bit to smile about, scoring her second goal to make it 8-2.

Seven defeats in a row, 38 goals conceded since the cup defeat at Upton Cross and drastic situations called for quick solutions.

The Facebook timelines of the girls showed the level of their desperation!

Some just put 'Help! Goalkeeper required!'

Maddy's was funnier though. She posted a photo of her goalkeeping gloves and said, "Anyone want to use these while I am suspended? Will wash them first!"

Leah was about to respond to a few of the posts. As captain she wanted to lead by example and keep the girls positive. But, everything she typed didn't sound right, so she kept pressing the delete key and starting over again.

In the end, she gave up, noticed her boyfriend was on line and popped up into chat to say "Hey x."

"Hey! Didn't think you would be on today," Luke replied.

"Yeah, Dad and Mum have taken Mikey to that new park, so I thought I'd pop onto the laptop while I got the chance."

"Cool. Seen some of your teammates Facebook posts?"

"Yeah, wanted to reply lol. But nothing seemed right. Hard to be positive when we have lost so many games!"

"Yup, know that feeling lol! Happened all the times at Deadtail until you came along, even with me in goal haha!"

"Modest!" Leah scoffed him.

"Haha, well all you need is a good goalkeeper while Maddy is out and you'll be fine!"

"Yeah, nineteen goals in two games says we haven't got one of them!"

"Yeah, I don't know of any either that haven't got a team already," Luke continued.

Leah sent a laughing emoji.

"What?" Luke asked.

"At training..." Leah typed. "Harry said something about you. Hannah and I thought he wanted you to do what I did and pretend to be eligible for our team!"

"Haha! I'm not wearing a skirt and sports bra for anyone!" Luke joked.

"We don't play in skirts!" Leah typed back quickly.

"Okay, okay!" Luke typed. "Trouble is, Lee, goalkeepers are a specialist position! People train years to be one."

"I know… pity we can't find someone who has been exposed to that training," Leah continued, sighing as she typed.

"I know someone who has had a couple of years' goalkeeping experience who can play for your team!" Luke messaged Leah quickly.

"Who?" Leah asked.

"Meet me at the park in twenty minutes."

"Okay!"

Chapter 6

Leah took longer than twenty minutes to get ready, so Luke was already at the park when she arrived.

She had expected Luke would be there with someone. Hopefully a six-foot teenager who could play in goal for Marshbrook. But he was alone.

Just Luke, in his football tracksuit and a football.

Leah hadn't exactly come dressed to play football! She had assumed she was meeting someone. So, a T-shirt and a pair of jeans wasn't exactly ideal gear for a kickabout.

"Erm... what's with the jeans?" Luke asked.

"You never said we were playing football!"

"Why else would we come to the park?"

"I thought we would be meeting a goalkeeper or something!"

"No!" Luke chuckled. "There's already a goalkeeper here!"

"Yeah, I know... you!" Leah said, mockingly.

"No, no, no!" Luke said.

"Then, who?"

Luke threw the ball towards Leah's stomach, which her reflexes caused her to catch.

"You, you numbskull!"

"Huh?"

"You said it on Facebook. About someone who has been exposed to goalkeeper training!"

"Uh-huh..."

"Well, **you** have! You have seen pretty much everything I've had to learn as a goalkeeper."

"Wait, wait a minute!" Leah exclaimed. "You are saying I should go in goal for Marshbrook?!"

Luke nodded.

"But..."

"You're the best player?" Luke interrupted.

"Well, er… yeah!" Leah said, somewhat shyly.

"But, what's the point?" Luke asked.

"What do you mean?"

"What's the point of having a great striker up front if you are conceding a goal every time the opponents have a shot? You aren't going to win 9-8 every week!"

"I don't even know if I am good enough!"

"Well, you can't be any worse!"

Leah chuckled.

"And," Luke continued. "You are captain. Lead by example. Tell the team you are doing this so the team don't lose any more matches. With a fighting spirit like yours, you'll have your teammates on your side!"

"Erm… okay. I guess we had better practise!"

They walked down towards their favourite part of the park where they regularly played football, with two trees far enough apart to be the goalposts of a football net.

"You wanna know how you will improve as a goalkeeper?" Luke asked.

"Go on…"

"Well…"

Luke kicked the ball towards the goal and it sailed past Leah and ran on forty metres or so beyond the trees. "The more shots you save, the less running you will have to do!"

Leah ran behind the goal to fetch the ball, but like Luke had said, she focused on saving as many of his shots as she could, from close range and long range, even saving a penalty or two!

"Not bad Boy Wonder!" Luke said.

"Cheers Kitten!" Leah replied.

Luke scoffed. "That nickname was two years ago now! I know why Harry called it me because of my cat-like agilities, but it's hardly an apt nickname for a young man!"

"Haha, young man!" Leah giggled, punching him playfully on the arm.

"Oi! Watch it! I don't want to be getting any arm injuries! I will play for England one day you know!"

"I don't doubt it," Leah said, smiling, rubbing Luke's arm better where she hand landed her 'punch' before linking arms and walking down to the café.

"I dunno if being a goalkeeper is a good idea though," Leah said, sipping from her glass of cola.

"Why?"

"I have Wembley soon! I'm more likely to get injured playing in goal by the ball whacking me than if I played outfield."

"Or less likely to! Less running, less likely to tear a muscle!"

"True!"

Leah smiled.

"Can't believe you're going to play at Wembley before me!" Luke said.

"It's hardly playing at Wembley! Just some ball juggling!"

"It's Wem-ber-ly!" Luke said slowly. "Just going there is amazing enough! You will get to walk on the famous turf that so many great players have played on!"

"Probably fall flat on my bum!" Leah laughed.

Leah couldn't think of Wembley just yet.

She had to tell Hannah she was volunteering to take over the goalkeeper's jersey for the return match with Woodmead.

Harry admired her captain's spirit. "Taking one for the team!" he said.

Hannah wasn't so sure but they also knew after a winless streak of results, it couldn't be any worse! The worst thing would be another big defeat before they welcomed Maddy back!

Woodmead's manager was quite shocked to see the team list when it was submitted to him and the referee.

"Your best player in goal, eh? You obviously don't want to score any goals today then!"

"We play to enjoy the game, don't we 'Annah?" Harry said, turning to his daughter.

Hannah thought it would be a good idea if they asked Luke to come along to the game, including him as part of the coaching team for the day. He agreed and spent the warm up testing Leah with some shots and catching practice to stretch her arms and muscles to their fullest.

They even used Daisy Ferguson to barge into her a few times to test Leah's physical strength under pressure. Leah stood up well to the task and looked like she had played in goal all her life! At least in the warm up, she did! The game itself would be a different matter.

"Test the keeper!" shouted the Woodmead manager. "She'll be rubbish!" he continued.

"May I remind you?" Harry said, in a very matter of fact manner. "These are children. They just want to play and enjoy themselves!"

"Nothing more enjoyable than winning, mate!" the manager replied, snidely.

"Believe me, there is!" Harry responded. "Believe me, there is!" he repeated.

Luke was stood next to his old manager while Hannah sat nervously watching the game unfold.

Woodmead tried a shot from the edge of the penalty area which flicked off the shin of Sarah and was heading towards the opposite corner to which Leah had already dived.

"GOAL!" shouted the Woodmead manager.

"Oh no!" shouted Luke, Harry and Hannah as one voice.

No you don't, thought Leah, somehow managing to twist her body and stick out her left leg. It wasn't much of a touch but she just about stretched the toes of her boot onto the ball, just enough to make the ball change direction. Just enough to make the ball hit the inside of the post and bounce back into Leah's grateful empty hands.

"Wahoo!" came several shouts from around the Marshbrook fans, players and managers.

Woodmead tried everything they could to unsettle Leah, standing in front of her at corner kicks, trying to block her path to the ball. But, however hard they tried, half-time came and Leah had still not been beaten by a shot and Maidens were holding on at 0-0.

Luke gave Leah the hugest hug at half-time but also kept her concentrated by saying, "The job's only half done!"

"I know!" Leah replied. "I do know how football works you Wally!"

Neither Hannah nor Harry had much to say to the players. They were clearly motivated enough to ensure there would be no repeat of the defeat of last week. They were motivated enough to protect Leah as best they could.

The visitors continued in the same manner and Leah remained resilient. Just like she had seen Luke do so many times before, she kept her eyes on the ball, got as much of her body behind it as she could and had a defiant, "You will not get past me!" attitude.

Woodmead made all of their substitutions, including changing their forwards to try and breakthrough the stubborn Maidens defence and the inspired number one.

Hannah looked at her watch. Two minutes left. Luke looked at Hannah's watch too!

Harry was shouting and bawling, "Come on m' gals!"

Marshbrook were defending as if their lives depended on it until the Woodmead number fifteen sprinted past Abby, who left a lazy leg hanging out and sent the substitute tumbling inside the penalty area.

The referee's whistle blew, the assistant put the flag across her chest and the referee pointed to the penalty spot. All that hard work could disappear in the space of seconds. One striker, one ball. Twelve yards. One so-called goalkeeper.

The purple-shirted Woodmead player placed the ball on the penalty spot and walked backwards to the white line on the edge of the penalty area.

Leah wanted to look across to Luke for advice but she knew there was no time. This was either going to be pure luck, instinct or a bit of both.

"What would I do?" she whispered. *Against a good goalkeeper I'd try and get it right in the corner. I think **any** goalkeeper would just pick a direction and dive to it*, she thought.

There was no time to think much more.

The referee put the whistle to her mouth and blew once to signify to continue.

The girl ran forward at quite a fast pace and just before her yellow boots made contact with the ball Leah looked the player in the eyes and a panic came over her and her decision to dive disappeared.

She just stood there. Rigid. Like a statue.

Thankfully for Leah, the striker had assumed Leah would dive and decided to go straight down the centre of the goal! The place Leah hadn't moved from.

The ball looped up slowly and even though Leah had been transfixed like a rabbit in the headlights of a car, the ball dollied nicely into Leah's hands. The easiest save she had ever made!

There was no time to celebrate though. There was probably still a minute of the game left so Leah tossed the ball up out of her hands and kicked it as far down the pitch as she could muster.

She didn't mind that the ball sailed over the heads of everyone and down towards the opposite corner flag. She had eaten up valuable seconds of the game. By the time Woodmead's goalkeeper had run out to keep the ball in play and kick it back up the pitch, the referee had blown the final whistle to an amazing goalless draw.

Harry held out his hand to shake it with Woodmead's manager. But he refused. "Told ya there was more to it than winning!" Harry said, gleefully.

Luke raced out onto the pitch to lift Leah off the ground in celebration.

"Get in! You beauty!" Luke shouted, lifting Leah's feet off the floor.

"Don't drop me!" Leah jested.

"I won't! I'm a goalkeeper!" Luke replied, laughing back.

"So am I!" said Leah.

Chapter 7

Since June, Leah had one date etched in her mind – November 29th. She had attended an England Ladies match and had been picked out of the crowd to take part in a keepy-uppy competition at half-time. A competition she had won.

Her prize was a trip to Wembley Stadium to compete against all of the other children who had won the other local challenges at the various matches.

It was a dream come true! Whatever else might happen in her career, however far it might progress, **no-one** would be able to take away the fact that she had played at Wembley Stadium!

No-one, except school.

The school were very proud of Leah's achievements and were delighted that the school was mentioned in the local newspapers when she had won the previous competition. They hoped they would be mentioned again and hoped that Leah would represent their school with some pride.

The Head Teacher even had a photo of himself doing keepy-uppies next to Leah when the newspaper reporter came to visit the school.

But, November 29th was a school day and they were **not** giving Leah permission to have the day off school to attend.

Leah wasn't told what the school had said. Her Mum had been in to see Leah's form teacher and stated that they were hoping to take Leah out of school the day before the Wembley event and the day after, to make a short holiday out of it.

The form teacher had explained the rules to Rose and said that Rose would need to speak to the Head Teacher to get permission.

The Head Teacher declined.

Rose could remember the exact words, as she retold them to Jeff that evening once Leah had gone to bed.

"Education is vital. If we give children days off to attend sporting events, it would open up a Pandora's Box of people wanting time off for their children. It would be impossible to control. It would be impossible to be fair to everyone."

To make it more official, the school even sent a letter to Jeff and Rose, a letter she showed to her husband the second he got home from work.

"Then that means she can't go!" Jeff replied disappointedly, understanding how Leah might have felt if she had known.

"I know!" Rose continued, "It'd be physically impossible to get to London after school in enough time for the match!"

"Would they even allow Leah to have the last lesson off giving us a bit of extra time to travel?"

"The Head said 'No' and seemed adamant that the rules could not be broken, even when Leah is, to quote him, 'Representing the school'!"

"She's not even representing the school!" Jeff said, in disgust. "She's representing herself and Marshbrook Maidens, if anyone!"

Rose nodded.

"Do you want me to speak to him?" Jeff asked.

"I doubt it would make any difference!"

"Hmmm…" Jeff muttered, as if he was searching for some inspiration!

Rose handed the letter from the school to Jeff. "The number's there if you want to give it a try but I wouldn't hold out much hope."

"I don't believe it!" Jeff squealed excitedly.

"What?!"

Jeff pointed to the list of names below the Head Teacher's name. A list of the school governors.

"So?" Rose asked.

"That one there…"

"Mr C. Kemper?"

"Yup!"

"And that is who?"

"Well, I doubt there's many Kempers in the phonebook. If it's who I think it is, then I used to work with Colin Kemper years ago. Saved him his job when he was being bullied by a co-worker."

Jeff paused to sip his coffee.

"This fella we worked with said he had been making several excessively long personal phone calls within work's time and not doing his work. Was his word against Colin's until I was checking our bank balance at lunch time and noticed our phone bill had gone out…"

"And?"

"Well, I asked him what sort of phone he had, whether he was pay as you go, contract, whatever and, you know, he never even realised he could go online to prove what phone calls had been made from his handset!"

"Ah!" Rose exclaimed, breaking up the monotony of Jeff talking.

"Yup! He proved he only made one phone call… of less than two minutes."

"He could have used the work phone," Rose pointed out.

"Nah, work had already checked them and he had been accused of using his mobile, which is against company policy!"

"Excellent!" Rose said. "And, do you still have this man's number, even if it is Colin Kemper?"

"Erm… no," Jeff said, flicking through his contacts on his phone.

Jeff looked glum.

"I'll find it somehow," he said, determinedly.

"No need!" Rose said.

"Huh?"

Rose turned her phone towards Jeff. "I have your old phone remember! Your old numbers are still on it."

Rose passed Jeff the phone and, once he had remembered how to text on it, typed out the message, "Hi Colin, wondering if you still have this number. Jeff Helmshore here. I don't suppose you are the Mr C. Kemper listed as a governor at the school our Leah goes to? Drop me a text back will you please, mate."

One hour had passed, then a second one. Leah's parents were giving up hope that this was Colin's phone number still.

During the television news, Jeff heard a faint sound from the kitchen. "Is that your phone?" he asked.

Rose was too settled on the sofa to move so she motioned an arm as if to say, 'Go and fetch it for me, servant!'

Jeff walked to the kitchen and removed the phone from the charger plugged into the wall and handed it to Rose.

"You could just have looked!" she said, lazily.

"Yeah true!"

Jeff unlocked the phone and lo and behold the text was from Colin.

"Hi mate," it read. "Yes, I'm a governor there. What can I do for you?"

Jeff started to type out the reply when the phone rang in his hand.

"Hi mate," Colin began. "Hope it's not too late to ring you. Thought it'd be easier than sending a load of texts back and forth."

Jeff knew that Leah would be unable to hear the phone conversation in her room, so he put the phone onto loud speaker so Rose could hear too.

"Hi Colin. It's a simple one really. Leah has been invited to go to…"

"Ah yes," Colin said, interrupting, "heard all about it! Well done. So proud of her!"

"But she can't go!"

"Why not?"

"It's a school day. The Head Teacher has written to say 'no'! That's where we saw your name."

"Ah okay, so you want me to chat to the other governors and overrule the Head, is that what you are saying?"

Jeff nodded, forgetting he was on the phone. "Erm… yes… cheeky, I know."

"Leave it with me. The next governor's meeting is tomorrow night, which is why I thought it best I rang you now when you asked about me being on the board."

"Thanks Colin. I'll text you my new number."

"Okay. Any time! Anything for a friend."

Leah was none the wiser to what was going on and returned from football training to see her Mum and Dad sat staring at the phone waiting for it to ring.

"Expecting someone?" Leah asked.

"Erm… we are just playing a game of Scrabble on it. I'm pondering my next move," Jeff answered.

Leah began to make her way upstairs to go to her room when the phone did ring. Leah paused halfway, lowered herself onto the step and turned an ear towards the kitchen.

It was Colin.

This time, Jeff realised that Leah could probably hear them so Rose and Jeff crowded closely to the phone to listen in.

"Hi mate," Colin said. "We've talked about it among the governors and we agreed that the Chairman of the Board of Governors will speak to the Head Teacher tomorrow to ask him to review his decision."

"Oh cool," Jeff replied.

"Can't promise anything but there was a child a couple of years ago in the sixth form who was allowed two days off to attend a trial for the Olympics. He only missed two lessons though with him being an A-level student, but we can cite that as an occasion where the Head – the same one – allowed it."

"Fingers crossed!" Rose exclaimed.

"Thanks Colin," Jeff said.

"Will let you know as soon as I do."

Rose tiptoed out of the kitchen while Jeff hung up the call. She had a sneaky feeling, as Mums do, that Leah was still there. She wasn't wrong.

"Were you listening in to our call?" Rose asked, somewhat sternly.

"No… erm… I didn't hear anything but I knew something important was going on."

"Nothing for you to worry about, love. Get yourself a shower to freshen up, if you didn't get one at football."

"Okay Mum."

The evening turned into morning and the morning into another Friday as Leah trudged off to school.

"Leah!" came a call from the Head Teacher as she walked through the school gate.

"Sir?"

"Can you make sure your parents get this letter tonight? Didn't want to post it as it will be Monday at least before they get it and it is rather important."

To say Leah was distracted all day would be an understatement. What was so important it couldn't wait until Monday? Or was the Head Teacher just saying that because he was too tight to put a stamp on it.

On several occasions during the day, Leah traced her finger over the seal of the envelope testing herself as to whether she could resist opening it or not.

Of course, she didn't. But it didn't mean that she didn't race home as fast as she could and prayed that her Mum didn't say, "Thank you dear, I'll open it when your Dad gets home."

Leah raced into the kitchen and hastily and breathlessly said, "Letter… school… important… open!"

Leah looked at her Mum as if to say, 'Please don't say wait until Dad is here.'

In truth though, Rose looked at the envelope, wondered for a split second whether she should wait for Jeff but realised she couldn't wait either!

She opened the envelope and pulled out and unfolded the A4 letter with the school logo on it.

"What is it?" Leah asked, excitedly.

Rose read it quietly and carefully. She wanted to make sure she hadn't misunderstood anything or missed a little word which changed the meaning of everything.

"Okay…" Rose hesitated, certain she had understood it fully.

"Well?"

"It's a letter from the school…"

"I know that… Duh!"

"...to say that it's okay for you to have time off school to go to Wembley!"

Rose looked ecstatic. Leah looked puzzled.

"Are you saying...?" Leah asked.

"Yes," said Rose calmly. Then, more excitedly said, "At first they said 'No' but your Dad knew someone on the Governors and they've changed their mind! We are going to London!"

Leah wasn't quite as excited as her Mum. In her mind, she had already known she was going! Nonetheless, she gave her Mum a huge hug, to which Mikey soon joined in.

"Can I come too?" Mikey asked.

"Oh –," said Rose. "We best check with Mikey's school too!

Chapter 8

Leah was delighted to finally turn the calendar page over to November, although the trip to Wembley was still four weeks away at the end of the month!

She couldn't help but play each Marshbrook match a little more cautiously, aware that one bad tackle, one over-stretch too many could cause an injury that would rule her out of what would surely be the greatest moment of her life so far!

Nevertheless, at the end of every school day, Leah took a thick red marker pen and crossed through each day of the month until the England match loomed ever closer.

The Football Association were very efficient with their requests of Leah and 'her party'.

As officials who were 'representing themselves, their team, their country and their sport' (according to the wording of the official letter) they were expected to wear official 'Guest' passes which were laminated plastic photograph IDs with an embroidered lanyard saying 'Official F.A. Guest' with the England Three Lions crest on it.

Jeff grabbed a yellow highlighter pen and was about to drag it across the paper to indicate something important when Leah screamed, "Noooooo!"

"What?" Jeff replied, stopping rapidly.

"Think Dad!"

"Erm…"

"I want to keep that letter forever! I don't want highlighter pen on it!"

Jeff's face showed embarrassment.

"What's the problem?" Rose enquired, entering the room when she heard the scream.

Jeff pointed.

Rose read out. "Where possible, participants involved in the keepy-uppy challenge are requested to wear either the football kit of the team they represent OR the new season full England kit. Asterisk…" Rose continued, "Which are available at a reduced price from the Football Association website for participants in this event, quoting KEEPY-UPPY1 as the voucher code."

"Pah! Trust them to make some money out of this!" Jeff grumbled.

"DAD!" Leah responded. "I'd rather wear my Marshbrook kit anyway. I'm sure there's one or two that aren't looking dog-eared yet!"

"True," Jeff acknowledged. "But perhaps not the substitute's shirts! No-one wants to see a number twelve on your back at Wembley! I am not having the world's eyes on my child thinking she's a reserve!"

"Lightbulb…" Leah said, smiling as an idea popped into her head.

"What?" her parents replied, simultaneously.

"You said 'no-one wants a number twelve'… what about if we got a brand new Marshbrook shirt with the number of keepy-uppies I did before!"

"Which was?" Jeff enquired, instantly regretting asking.

"203!" Leah and Rose said at the same time, both glaring at Jeff as if to say, "What do you mean you didn't remember!?"

Leah was on the case, quickly texting Hannah to see how quickly they could get a replica Marshbrook shirt and if it could accommodate three digits printed on the back, with Leah's name of course!

They could! And, a few days before the Wembley trip, Leah proudly held up the brand new shirt with her name and number on, which her Dad photographed straight away and had it on social media sites in no time!

The Helmshores hadn't been on holiday that summer so Jeff thought it would be a great weekend, albeit a cold November, to take them all away to London for a few days.

After a long journey on the motorway, with Leah losing count of the number of times Mikey asked, "Are we there yet?" they eventually checked into their rooms for the night and settled down for a good night's sleep. They had seen Wembley Stadium from the car on the journey which just made everyone that little bit more excited.

None of them had been to London before so they had to do lots of googling to find out whether places were walkable or which Tube station they needed to go to.

Eventually, after lots and lots of discussions, they found out they needed to get to Baker Street station, which got them talking so much about Sherlock Holmes that they missed the first train and had to wait for the next one!

Mikey didn't know where they were going, but Leah did and they got off the Underground, made their way back up to street level and looked for the signs.

Jeff was an organised man and had worked out two days previously that he had wanted to go to the mystery location and had booked tickets to avoid the queue to pay on the day.

"We're here!" Leah exclaimed.

"Mad-Amy-Tuss-Ads?" Mikey read out, spelling it in his head.

"Madame Tussauds!" Rose said, correcting him.

"What the?" asked Mikey.

"You'll see!"

They entered through the door signposted as 'Advanced ticket holders' although Leah cheekily suggested that they should enter through the 'VIP entrance'!

Down a couple of stairs into a large room, their eyes focused on a room full of people taking photos of what Mikey thought were other people!

"Don't stand still for too long!" Leah joked.

"Why?" asked Mikey.

"They'll think you are one of the wax statues!" she sniggered.

"Oh!" said Mikey, realising. "These aren't real people?"

"The ones that aren't moving are dummies, you dummy!" Leah chuckled.

"They are sculptures, Leah!" Rose said, correcting her daughter this time.

"But who are they meant to be?" asked Mikey.

"Famous people," Rose stated.

"Who's this one?" Mikey asked.

"I don't know," Rose replied.

"Not very famous then is he!" Mikey said, smugly.

Leah didn't recognise some of them either, but she did recognise the sculptures of Doctor Who, the Royal Family, James Bond, Michael Jackson, Elvis Presley and the Beatles.

Mikey only recognised the Queen (although he thought her name was Victoria) and called all the sports people David Beckham and then didn't say David Beckham's name when it actually was him!

Jeff's phone rang while they were in Tussauds but he didn't answer it as he didn't recognise the number.

The same number rang again half an hour later (which he also ignored). But when it rang a third time, he answered, concluding it must be important.

It was a representative from the Football Association, checking that Leah had arrived for the Wembley challenge and that she had all the correct clothing "as per our letter," the man said.

Jeff did lots of nodding, even though he was on the phone and couldn't be seen!

He motioned to Rose to pass him a pen and started writing a few things down on a scrap piece of paper that Rose had fished out of her handbag.

Leah peered and tried to look around her Dad's shoulder as she wasn't yet tall enough to look over it. He had written down what Leah assumed to be the name of the road they needed to meet on, the time they were meant to meet and the name of the lady who would greet them.

Back in the hotel, Leah couldn't sleep. She had always dreamed of playing for England. Dreamed of playing at Wembley.

Okay, so this wasn't a match for her country, but it was possibly as close as she would ever get!

Her parents had always told her to try not to worry, to try and always be positive. But, she always had that little niggling thought at the back of her head that said, "What if?"

What if the car breaks down on the way to Wembley? What if I get injured warming up? What if I fall over and make a complete fool of myself? What if I don't do a single keepy-uppy?

Nothing was settling her, so she plugged in her headphones, switched on her phone's radio player and tried to listen to something that made her relax. In the end she fell asleep.

Rose came to wake her the following morning and Leah felt reasonably refreshed. A good breakfast of muesli, a banana for energy and a glass of orange juice and Leah was full of beans, except she hadn't had any beans!

Rose checked the times of the trains to Wembley Stadium (as Jeff didn't fancy driving through London either) and they allowed themselves an extra hour to have a quiet cuppa and a sandwich when they arrived.

On arrival, they soon discovered that the keepy-uppy challenge was no longer at half-time. When the Football Association staff had talked about it, they realised that if everyone did around two hundred keepy-uppies (as they had done before) that it would take a lot longer than the interval of fifteen minutes.

The competitors and their families were given a bit of a guided tour of the stadium surroundings and a pep talk of Dos and Don'ts of representing England at the 'Home of Football.'

Leah got to meet the nine other children she was up against, as two of the twelve regional winners were unable to attend. Leah wondered if it was because their schools hadn't allowed them to attend.

She was sure it wasn't deliberately like that, but there were five girls and five boys including herself, ranging from the age of twelve to the age of sixteen.

They had to introduce themselves to the rest of the group, say who they played for (if anyone), where in the country they had travelled from and how many keepy-uppies they had done to reach Wembley.

The lowest had been 120 and the highest 295. If Leah had listened carefully enough and worked it out right then she had come seventh out of the ten.

She made it a challenge to herself to try and come in the top five.

All ten of them were asked to put their hand into a velvet bag, the actual one (or so Alan from Middlesbrough said) that they use to do the F.A. Cup draw.

In turn, they picked out a numbered ball, determining which order they would take to the Wembley turf.

Leah was whispering in her head, *not one, not one, not one!*

The lady from the F.A. said that they would choose in order of the lowest score to reach the final, which meant Leroy picked first and it appeared that he felt the same as Leah, cheering when he picked out number six.

Enola picked five, then Candice drew out number four.

Leah was next and nervously slipped her hand into the bag, still thinking, *not one, not one!*

"Two!" she exclaimed, relieved.

Ethan, Erin, Alan then Rianna also avoided going first, though Erin wasn't keen on being the tenth contestant either.

That left Stevie and Jacob, with Stevie the unlucky lad (and the youngest at twelve) to go first. Though, he just shrugged his shoulders said, "Gets it over with!" and smiled nervously.

The boys and girls were separated into two side offices to get changed and were raring to go as soon as the door was knocked to tell them it was their moment.

They walked nervously out into a crescendo of noise inside Wembley Stadium, glad they didn't know exactly how many people were watching! The ground wasn't yet full, which was both an advantage and disadvantage of performing before the game started. However many people were watching wasn't as high as how many there could have been!

The Public Announcer introduced them all one by one and Stevie was handed a ball and began to perform a repertoire of keepy-uppies.

Eventually, Stevie fell short of his 293 from his previous attempt, ending on 222.

The announcer introduced Leah and she was handed a football, making sure she didn't do anything silly like dropping it before she even started!

Leah's first few kicks were tentative and nervous. She didn't want to mess this up and only do a dozen or so and then fall flat on her back!

But, once she had overcome that initial nervousness, Leah had almost forgotten where she was and just focused on keeping the ball off the ground and chalking off each ten in her head until she reached one hundred and then onto two hundred.

She was delighted to pass the 203 number on her shirt and was getting over-excited as she headed towards 250, eventually falling short on 245!

She could hear the applause ringing around the stadium as the announcer praised her for her total. As quick as her moment of fame was at its highest though, it was quickly onto Alan and that fleeting moment of applause for her had become Alan's moment in the spotlight.

Alan's juggling skills came to an end on 211 while Candice raced to a hundred but quickly saw the ball bounce off the lush Wembley turf on 160.

Next up, Enola was giving Leah a great battle. She moved smoothly up to three figures and then two hundred but then slipped trying to retrieve a header and Leah had beaten her, ending on 239.

Knowing that she was ahead after five competitors, Leah knew that she had done better than she had done before and that one more person failing to beat her would mean she finished in the top half.

It wasn't a feeling that sat comfortably with her though. She had always been brought up to be a part of a team, wanting the best for everyone. It did seem strange wanting the others to fail so that she would succeed.

The remaining group contained the original winner, Jacob and Rianna who had come third. So, Leah knew her chances of winning were probably slim.

Leroy was doing well until he glanced round at what the noise was as the England Ladies players came onto the field to warm up and that split-second loss of concentration was his downfall.

Rianna also reached two hundred but ended on 217 and Ethan got even closer to Leah's total, notching 236, just nine short.

"Top three!" Leah thought to herself, smiling so wide that the arch above Wembley could probably have fitted within her smile!

The announcer looked a little nervous as the kick off time for the match was getting ever nearer.

Next up, was Jacob. The favourite.

Leah had made a mental note when they were all introduced to one another that he was the one who had got nearly three hundred to reach this final.

Leah's eyes were fixed upon him. 237, 238. *Drop it* she thought but didn't want to say it out loud.

239, 240.

It was all happening very quickly and Leah had a second thought, contrasting her first one. She glanced at her surroundings the Wembley arch shining above her and suddenly she didn't care whether Jacob beat her or not.

241, 242, Leah began to clap her hands in rhythm with the rest of the crowd.

243, 244, Leah was enjoying herself too much to even remember whether she was winning or not.

245, 246, Jacob had won but Leah thrust both her arms into the air in celebration at how well Jacob had done, catching up with the incredible atmosphere of the occasion.

"We have a new leader!" screamed the announcer.

Minutes later when Wolverhampton's Erin lost control of the ball on 232, the announcer put the microphone to his lips once more and said, "Ladies and gentlemen, boys and girls, our winner, Jacob from Newcastle!"

The ten were applauded as they were ushered quickly from the field, aware of the imminent kick off of the England match.

Unfortunately, they didn't get to see any of the first half of the match as they were too busy recovering from their experience. All of them were proud of what they had just done.

The lady from the F.A. came into the room where they were all gathered.

"Thank you ever so much for that!" she exclaimed. "Richly entertaining, and the crowd loved you."

There were ten faces beaming with pride looking back at her.

"The day's not quite over for you all," she continued. "We would like you back on the field at half-time as we have medals to present to you all."

"Wow!"

"Awesome!"

They made their way out toward the Wembley pitch centre-circle one more time, Jacob leading the way, Leah just behind.

One by one, beginning with the tenth-placed Candice, they bowed their heads as a shiny silver-coloured medal was placed around their necks attached to a white and red ribbon.

Once fourth-placed Ethan had received his, the announcer spoke again.

"Ladies and gentleman, receiving a bronze medal (which Leah noticed was larger than the other medals given out so far), from Ludlow, Shropshire, give it up for Enola!"

By now, the ground was probably at its maximum attendance, the few thousand who had made their way to snack bars at half-time having begun returning to their seats.

"In second, receiving a silver medal, Leah Helmshore!"

It was unlikely that she actually did, but Leah was sure she heard Mikey hollering, "That's my sister!"

"And in first place, receiving a gold medallion, Jacob!"

The ground erupted with noise, partly to applaud Jacob but mostly as it coincided with England's players returning to the field of play, 1-0 up from their first half endeavours.

The ten were shepherded back towards the offices where they previously were and taken through a series of corridors to where their families were sat.

Leah shuffled past a few people who were already sat there and parked herself between her Mum and Dad.

Before she had time to speak, her parents had an arm each around her and Mikey planted a huge kiss on his sister's forehead!

"You were proud of me, then?" she asked, her voice muffled by the hugs of her family.

"Just a bit!" her Dad said.

"You could've won if you tried harder!" Mikey joked.

"Mikey!"

"Only joking!" he chuckled. "I like the medal! Can I try it on?"

Leah placed it over her brother's neck who, from that moment, didn't see any of the second half of the game. He spent the whole 45 minutes looking at his face reflected in the silver medal.

"I want to be a footballer!" Mikey said, turning to his Dad.

Chapter 9

Leah twisted and turned in her bed. Something was unsettling her and she woke up startled, questioning for a second where she was!

She sat upright and spun her legs out from under the crisp, white duvet and used her feet to feel for her slippers before sliding them in.

She had a knack of restless nights after a football match. Her Mum had suggested it was an adrenalin rush, speeding up her heart rate, making it harder for her to slow down again and rest.

But, she hadn't played football since the weekend and it was several days since she had played at Wembley.

"I must still be excited from that," she said quietly, aware of Mikey in the adjacent room (although he was snoring away and it would take more than a restless big sister to wake him up).

She was still half asleep, rubbed her eyes and wiggled a little finger in her ear. She could hear Mum and Dad talking quite loudly downstairs. Maybe that was what woke her.

Leah was tempted to tell them to keep the noise down but, instead, she opened her bedroom door slightly.

She stepped back into her room. Startled.

It was clear that the loud talking was actually arguing!

She felt embarrassed to have overheard, but also curious what they were arguing about.

Of course, like most families, all the Helmshores had their moments when they were a bit cranky – getting confused by the directions of the satnav and missing an important turning was the biggest one.

But Leah had never heard **anything** like this.

She desperately needed the toilet. But that would have to wait.

Curiosity got the better of her. She wanted to listen. **Needed** to listen. So she parked herself on the top step of the stairs and remained as quiet as an empty football ground.

Although the voices were loud, they were muffled by the closed kitchen door. Rose and Jeff had made sure of that.

Leah was only able to pick out the occasional word – money, haircuts, job, were three she picked out but wasn't really able to fully link them together.

She stood up ready to go to the bathroom and the top step of the stairs creaked loudly.

"Sshh!" Leah said to the step, as if it could hear her or do anything about creaking.

She was convinced it had creaked enough that her Mum and Dad had heard her as the talking in the kitchen came to a sudden halt.

The noise from the kitchen remained silent for ten, twenty, thirty seconds, probably a couple of minutes – or at least it felt like it, sitting down again, getting rather cold and increasingly in need of the bathroom.

Leah gave up waiting for the conversation (the argument) to start again. She went to the toilet quietly, returned to her bed and before too long she fell asleep (the second her head touched the pillow).

The birdsong alarm tone on her phone woke her up promptly at seven and, surprisingly bright as a button, Leah hurtled off to take a shower and then into the kitchen for her breakfast where her Mum was pouring a cup of tea and her Dad was sat at the table with his laptop open.

"Morning Mum! Morning Dad! No work today?" Leah said cheerily.

There was a deathly hush.

"Leah…" Rose said, "Sit down, before Mikey gets here."

Leah sat down and looked puzzlingly at her parents.

Rose continued, "There's been a fall in sales at your Dad's work. They needed to cut some jobs. Your Dad found out yesterday that he was one of those to go."

"Just like that? No warning?"

"We've known a while, pet," Jeff said, softly. "We just wanted to keep it from you in case I was one of the lucky ones that kept their job."

"Hence the laptop," Rose asserted. "The job hunt starts immediately."

"I'll have a redundancy payment at the end of the month," Jeff said, reassuringly. "Will get us a nice little holiday if I have found a job by then. But, until then, we might just have to tighten the purse strings a bit to make ends meet."

"I... er... did hear a few words last night when I went to the bathroom," Leah said, honestly.

"What did you hear?"

"Er... 'Money'... 'Haircuts'... 'Job'... I guess I worked out two of the words now, but what have haircuts got to do with anything?" Leah asked.

Calmly, Jeff replied, "Your Mum's can cost around £40 or £50 and I always let the barber keep the change from a tenner when I pay for mine. It was just a discussion where we could make savings that's..."

Jeff didn't finish his sentence as Mikey came bustling into the kitchen demanding his cereal.

Leah looked at her Dad as if to say, 'When are you telling Mikey?' and Jeff must have read her mind answering, "After school."

Understandably, Leah's mind was pre-occupied throughout the school day.

She'd never known her Dad not have a job. She had plenty of friends whose parents didn't have jobs and she knew how rarely they went to the cinema or had nice stuff at Christmas. Leah knew she had been very fortunate.

In fact, the first few days of having Dad at home in the morning was fantastic. Jeff walked Mikey to and from school and had time on his hands after school to have a kick about in the garden with Leah and Mikey.

"I don't want you to get another job!" Mikey said, proudly.

"We need money der brain!" Leah replied, taunting her younger brother.

"Yeah, we do Mikey!" Jeff cut in. "I don't miss the 75 minutes travelling to work and the even longer journey home, but I will miss the wages!"

"You'll get a job soon!" Leah stated positively.

But, one week turned into two, two weeks turned into three and three into a month as email after email came into Jeff's inbox saying he was 'Unsuccessful' this time.

Jeff had worked there forever. Leah had heard him say he would get a "tidy sum of money" as a redundancy payment but had also heard Mum say "it won't last forever."

Rose had not worked since Leah had been born and she too was scanning the job pages for some work, just in case Jeff kept being unlucky in his own quest to find a new job.

Leah had noticed already that things had changed in the household. The normal Friday night takeaway had gone. She was old enough to realise that other things might get cut out too.

Mikey's treat of after-school club twice a week was also cut from the budget and by week three of Jeff's unemployment the kids and movie channels were taken off their Sky box.

Leah was worried that the football would be the next to go. Even though she only paid a few pounds every week for the use of the training facilities, the petrol costs to away matches in particular could easily be classed as non-essential spending.

On top of this, Mikey had also expressed a desire to go to football training and Leah was worried that he would be allowed to pursue that hobby at Leah's expense.

She didn't know whether she should tell Hannah, but she knew she could confide in Harry.

"What if Dad and Mum stop me coming to football if we can't afford it?"

"It won't come to that, Leah!" Harry replied. "Don't stop believing that they will find work soon. And... if they don't then we'll talk about it..."

Leah nodded.

Harry continued, "I mean, come on Leah, do you really think all them lads at Deadtail Dragons could afford to come every week?"

Leah hadn't really thought about it.

"We 'ad a bit of a grant from the Authority, to be truthful, so we never needed the money from all the kids. But, you may think it unfair, but yeah while some of you were paying, some of them never did."

"Oh."

"Of course money makes the world go round, but no-one should be stopped from following their dream 'cause they 'aven't got the pennies to pay for it."

"Thanks Harry!" Leah said, reassured.

Nothing in life was that simple though.

At the next Marshbrook game, thankfully with Maddy now back in goal, an over-zealous tackle saw the blades on the bottom of the Brightwood Belles player scrape down the main part of Leah's boots making a slight rip in the synthetic material – a tear that got bigger as the match progressed.

"You wouldn't get that with the football boots I wore!" Jeff exclaimed.

'Back in my day,' Leah mouthed, out of eyesight of her Dad.

"Do you even have another pair?" he asked.

"Not that fit!" Leah replied, close to tears, though she was holding them back well so far.

"Well, you can't play with no boots!" Jeff said, stating the obvious.

"I know!"

"And we can't buy new boots with no money!"

"I know that too!"

Leah did begin to cry.

"So, what can I do? Even if I did all the jobs around the house, you can't pay me pocket money, can you?"

"No, I can't."

"But Dad! Football means everything to me!"

"A roof over our heads means everything to all of us!" Jeff responded.

"We're not that badly off for money, are we?" Leah asked.

"No, we're not. But we do have to prioritise now."

"And...?"

"Boots aren't a priority!" Jeff said.

Leah's heart sank.

Chapter 10

Leah cried on her bed.

She stared at the one damaged boot, which she couldn't think to throw away just yet and looked at the other boot, in perfectly good condition.

It made things worse when she saw on Facebook, a Premier League club posting a photo from inside the dressing room before the game and each player had four or five pairs of boots set out beneath their changing space.

"I wonder if anyone has ever worn that many pairs of boots in one game!" she exclaimed.

She didn't want to tell Hannah nor Harry just yet that she might not be able to play at the weekend. She had other ideas first.

Step one was to text all of her teammates. There was bound to be someone with the same size foot as her that could lend her a pair of boots for the weekend.

One by one the replies filtered back.

"Sorry."

"No, I have big feet."

"Nope, I'm not a size six."

"I did have some, but Mum gave them to a 'Football Boots for African Children' scheme the other week. Sorry chick."

She even text her boyfriend Luke to see if he knew anyone with a spare pair lying around somewhere.

No joy there either.

"It looks like the end of your football season," he replied.

"Yup, the final whistle has blown," she texted back.

She looked at the somewhat grubby socks on her feet.

"Where am I going to get the money to buy new boots from?"

Leah didn't have a bank account. Her Mum and Dad were always generous with pocket money so she pretty much got whatever she wanted, without ever being spoiled.

She was also allowed to keep the change when she did little bits of shopping for her Mum. Leah looked at the pink piggy bank on the dresser by her bed but there wouldn't be enough money in there to buy a pair of football boots.

Or was there?

She leapt off her bed and sprung across the room to the piggy bank, turned it upside down on her quilt and pulled out the black rubber stopper.

Turning it back the right way round, she gave it a shake and watched the coins slowly tumble out.

At first, there was a bit of excitement as a few gold coloured pound coins tumbled out, then came a few tens and fifties but then a batch of dull, brown, boring copper coins.

She tried to guess how much was there. She reckoned £15 if she was lucky. She slowly and methodically started to count.

"Pounds first!" she said, confidently.

She ferreted around amongst the coins on her duvet and got excited to pull out nine pound coins, which she stacked neatly on the bedside cabinet.

"Decent start!" she said, smiling.

There were a handful of fifties and twenties, just short of another £5 worth of those.

Feeling dejected, she piled up the tens, fives, twos and pennies. If she had added it up right, the grand total was £16.04.

Even if she went to the cheapest football boot shop in town, she would struggle to get a pair of boots for that!

Mikey burst into the room to see the ceramic pig on the bed and the money piled up in front of the bedside lamp.

"What are you doing?" he asked.

"Counting my money."

"Why?"

"To see how much I have got."

"Why?"

"To see if I have enough to buy a pair of football boots."

"Why?"

Leah pointed to the ripped boot on the carpet.

"That's why!"

"How much do you need?"

"I dunno," Leah said.

"So, why are you counting your money if you don't know how much you need? How will you know if you have enough?"

"Erm... I dunno Mikey."

"Hang on..."

Mikey ran out of the room and into his bedroom, returning immediately with his own money box – a bright yellow Lego one.

"You can have my money!" he declared.

"As if you have money!" Leah said, surprised.

Leah didn't seem very confident when Mikey handed it to her. It certainly didn't make a lot of noise when she rattled it.

Mikey needed Leah's help to get it open but eventually managed it and he sat on the bed in front of Leah, ready to pour out the contents.

Leah wasn't hopeful and wasn't anticipating much to come out.

She was right.

Barely twenty pence in coppers and a one pound coin tumbled out onto the bed.

"Is that it?" Leah asked. "I couldn't even buy some new laces with that!"

"It's all the coins I have!" Mikey replied.

"Thanks for the offer, bro!" Leah said, smiling, leaning over to give Mikey a hug.

Mikey took the money box back off his sister and put his fingers into the hole at the bottom.

"What are you doing?" Leah asked.

"There's one of these in here too," he said, pulling out a bank note slowly.

"A tenner!" Leah shouted, startled.

"Yeah, Aunty Miriam gave it me for my last birthday. I just put it in there for a rainy day like she told me to."

"It's raining now alright!" Leah said.

Mikey looked puzzled, glancing towards the large window in Leah's room.

"The sun is shining!" he declared.

"It was an expression!" Leah said, slapping her forehead with her hand, wondering why she even tried to explain things to her brother.

"Oh."

"I meant," Leah tried to explain. "You had to save it for a rainy day. For when you needed it. Well, I need it. Did you really mean I could have it?"

"Yes, I meant it," Mikey answered.

"So, that's sixteen plus ten plus that pound you had too. Twenty-seven pounds. Might just be enough."

Leah threw her arms around Mikey, gave him a kiss on the forehead and frantically started searching for boots on the internet on her phone.

'Football boots size 6 girls' she typed in quickly, clicking on the magnifying glass to begin her search.

Five images came up at the top of the page before all the other links further down. Two were actually training shoes rather than boots, one pair of boots were £32 and two were twenty.

Knowing she could now afford either, she chose the ones she wanted according to the colour – fluorescent yellow with a pink tick on them.

Leah smiled, gathered up the money and raced down to the sports shop in the High Street before it closed. She wasn't going to wait until tomorrow in case Mikey changed his mind, or if her Dad or Mum told her not to.

Before she knew it, she was back in her bedroom, holding the boots in her hand, imagining what fortune they might bring her in the weekend's match.

Chapter 11

Leah wasn't sure if she believed in luck or not, but she didn't think her new pair of boots were as good as her last pair!

In the return match with Morburn, her shooting was so bad that Abby Moore, who scored two goals in the 4-2 win, suggested **she** should go up front for the next game and Leah should be a defender instead!

That was followed by another defeat to Stony Hollow, before Marshbrook Maidens finally got some consistent form back together again with three wins in a row, 4-2 over Wellington, 2-1 over Nailsworth and 4-3 over Farthinghoe.

Zara Perry had scored in three games in a row, Daisy Ferguson had scored in four games in a row.

Leah, after five games in her new boots, hadn't scored a single goal and hadn't scored since the game before she deputised for Maddy in goal against Woodmead!

In those five weeks, Jeff still hadn't found a job, but Rose had, stacking shelves and working on the tills in the local supermarket. It came in handy with the food shopping too with a discount card for working there, meaning for now at least Leah was still given her money every week to go to football training.

The Wagstaff management team were happy with the recent results though with Marshbrook sitting comfortably in the middle of the league table.

In fact, after the Farthinghoe victory, Harry had a chat with the girls to say that "'is job was done" and that, "'Annah can carry on without me now you lot are winning games again."

Hannah was sorrowed that her Dad wasn't going to be her right hand man any more, but was grateful for his help.

Away from her Dad's earshot, she gathered the girls together to discuss some sort of farewell party after the next training session – maybe a meal at one of those buffet diners with a zillion different dishes to choose from.

A mild winter turned into a bitter spring and the next two training sessions had to be cancelled due to snow as well as the next two matches.

Harry had agreed though that he wouldn't step down as assistant until after the next game, whenever that would be.

Eventually the snow thawed and Hannah was able to text the girls that training would resume on the Thursday night, reminding them that they would go out for a meal afterwards to say goodbye to Harry properly.

It was a bitterly cold night and a few of the girls had wimped out of training to stay in the warmth of their living rooms!

Just eight girls turned up, so with Hannah and Harry there they just about had enough for a quick five-a-side match to keep warm, with Harry and Hannah taking on the roles of goalkeeper as the oldest two there.

The grass pitches were frozen solid so they moved to the artificial surface next to the car park where, not surprisingly, very few people had turned out to play.

"Thanks for coming girls," Hannah said. "We'll keep it short because of the weather but it'll be a shame not to have a bit of a match as we've made the effort to come."

"Us five," said Harry "against you five."

"Sounds good!" Hannah replied. "Let's get started!"

Leah had definitely come prepared for the late winter chill, with thick black gloves, a co-ordinated black scarf wrapped round her neck and a beanie hat on her head. Even after fifteen minutes of play, the hat, scarf and gloves stayed on!

Harry's team did everything they could to prevent Hannah's team from getting shots at goal, knowing full well that the rather rotund figure of Mr Wagstaff would not have been able to move too much to stop the ball entering the goal!

However, Harry did fill up more of the goal than the skinnier Hannah did!

The game began at a slow pace as the players got used to the skiddy pitch and the cold conditions, carefully and precisely controlling the ball and passing to a player on the same side.

In time though, Hannah quickened it up by saying that each player could only touch the ball a maximum of two times before another player touched it. Later, this increased to one touch football and they had to pass the ball on the second it reached them!

This got the blood flowing and the heart rate quickening and even some of the players threw down their gloves and hats as they were getting that bit warmer!

Leah was getting a little bit puffed out with all the running around in the cold air which was making her breathless, a problem she had encountered before with her asthma. She asked if she could swap with Harry in goal for a little breather, to which Mr Wagstaff replied immediately.

"It would be my 'onour!"

"Thanks Harry!" Leah responded breathlessly.

"Life in the old dog yet, you know!" Harry beamed confidently, exchanging quick passes with Maddy Baker, who wasn't in goal for a change!

Harry was dashing around the pitch like a terrier dog chasing the ball, creating space for the girls and making sure he led by example of how to outplay the opponent.

He received the ball off Maddy one more time and curled a right foot shot towards the goal which Hannah didn't even move towards, as the ball made a tinny pinging noise on the inside of the goal post and rolled into the white netting.

"By 'eck! First goal for twenty years!" Harry exclaimed gleefully.

He raced back towards his goal to high five Leah.

"Move over, Lee! I ain't gonna score another in my life time. Time for a rest."

The game continued at pace with goals scored at one end, then over at the other end. In truth, everyone lost count of the score and after a few minutes of 'Next goal is the winner!' resulted in no-one else scoring, Hannah put her whistle to her lips and blew for full-time.

"Let's call it a draw!" Harry cried out, a little out of breath still from his goal some minutes before.

"Wrap up warm girls. Meet us in the coffee area and we'll warm up with a hot chocolate or something," Hannah instructed. "We'll collect all the stuff in."

"I'll do it 'Annah!" Harry said, calmly. "You go pay for all them drinks. I'll be done in no time."

The leisure centre staff knew Hannah and the Marshbrook Maidens very well, so they knew the second Hannah got to the till she'd pay for all the girls drinks, so they happily carried on serving the eight girls until Hannah arrived.

She put her bag on the floor next to Leah and popped to the toilet before going to settle the bill.

Looking towards Louise on the till, she asked, "I'll have a cappuccino please. Dad, what do you want?"

"He's not here yet, Hannah," Daisy said.

"Oh, okay... he only had a few cones and balls to collect in. He's probably on the phone to Mum about his goal! Would one of you run and ask him what drink he wants?" Hannah asked, turning to the two tables of girls.

Daisy was the first to bolt upright and dash out to the Astroturf. At first, her sprint was quick, but slowed down with hesitancy as she surveyed the scene and noticed there was no-one standing on the pitch.

"Mr Wagstaff?" she called, before gently trotting forward, her head moving from side to side trying to spot where Harry's car was and whether he was standing next to that, or maybe even sat in it on the phone as Hannah had surmised.

She spotted his car and dashed over to it. The windscreen had frozen over slightly, as had the driver's side window, but when she brushed away the dusty ice that had begun to form, it was clear that no-one was in the car.

Call it women's intuition or a stroke of good fortune, but she felt something inside her that told her to look back towards the pitch, even though she knew she hadn't seen anyone standing on it.

"Oh Sh-! Harry! HANNAH!"

Chapter 12

Daisy didn't know which way to run.

She saw the figure of Harry lying in a heap on the floor.

Did she run to him or run to Hannah?

As fast as she could she ran back to the coffee shop.

"HANNAH! Quick!"

Daisy sprinted off, the other girls followed afterwards, as well as one of the leisure centre workers who carried a walkie talkie, rapidly overtaken by Hannah, taking the phone out of her pocket just in case.

As they approached the figure of Harry crumpled up on the floor, it became obvious that he wasn't moving and the leisure centre worker quickly dialled 999 to request an ambulance.

Hannah had some basic first aid training but she had never been in a situation like this. Not with anyone. Certainly not her own Dad.

She frantically loosened the tracksuit top Harry was wearing. She had to do something, even if she wasn't sure what she should be doing.

The words Hannah was uttering wouldn't have made a lot of sense by themselves. "Ambulance. When? Where?"

The man from the leisure centre knelt down next to Harry. Leah could see his name badge said Ed.

Ed pushed back the sleeve of Harry's top to check for a pulse.

"Miss…" Ed said, looking up at Hannah, "I don't think the ambulance will help," trying to motion the Marshbrook players away from the scene.

"What? Ambulance. Where?"

"He's not breathing. We're already too late."

Hannah cried.

The flashing blue light in the distance shone through the trees and got increasingly brighter as the ambulance sped its way into the leisure centre grounds, slowing only to negotiate the speed bumps in the 5mph pedestrian zone.

The ambulance crew raced towards the scene with a stretcher in hand and bent down over Hannah, Ed and Harry.

The girls had silently backed away, some numb in shock, some trying hard to hold back the tears. Leah was numb.

Ed returned to the coffee area and organised more drinks for the girls, who were now waiting to be collected by their parents. Not that any of them were leaving until they were told the inevitable words. The leisure centre staff weren't concerned if anyone would pay for them or not. Not right now anyway.

It seemed like an age before Hannah came into the coffee area, a silver foil blanket wrapped around her shoulders to keep her warm. A female member of the ambulance crew had her arm around Hannah's shoulder.

Ed walked over and shepherded the two of them to a private office. He accompanied them into the room but it wasn't long before he was out again.

He walked over to the group of girls just as the first couple of parents arrived.

He didn't need to speak. The girls looked up at him. Ed, with a sorrowful expression, curled his top lip over his bottom lip, bowed his head and nodded.

Eventually he did gulp back and whisper, "He's gone."

Leah stood and walked to the office and knocked the door. She didn't wait for a reply, pulling down the handle quietly and gently, before stepping in, closing the door behind her.

The ambulance lady looked up as if to say, "Leave her alone, please" but Hannah looked up shortly afterwards and sobbed, "Oh Leah!"

The two hugged, the tears streamed down Hannah's icy cold cheeks.

The door creaked slightly as the paramedic left the room, returning briskly with a coffee for Hannah.

Hannah slurped the top of the drink before another timid knock at the door was heard.

"Dad!" Leah howled, as Jeff walked in.

He hugged his daughter and placed a hand on Hannah's shoulder.

"Anything I can do?"

"Ring Mum... please," Hannah whispered, passing Jeff her phone.

Jeff took the phone and noticed a door opposite where he entered, leading to another small office, darkened by a blind on the window.

He pulled the door closed behind him.

Leah and Hannah couldn't hear what was said but they knew the call was short and concise.

"She's on her way over," Jeff said, calmly. "She's going to ask Bill, I think she said, to bring her."

"Their neighbour," Hannah stated.

Jeff really wasn't sure what else to say. But he realised he needed to say, "Hannah, I am so, so sorry. Anything we can do, you just have to say!"

Hannah didn't move a muscle. She couldn't even bring herself to thank Jeff for the offer or for ringing her Mum.

Jeff and Leah left Hannah alone for a while and returned to the coffee shop which had emptied considerably from earlier that evening.

Some of the Maidens had waited with their parents until Leah or Jeff had come back out of the office. It hadn't seemed right for them to go home until they had seen Leah again.

Jeff spoke inaudibly to a few of the other parents. Then followed, a lot of hand shaking and patting on the back until in twos and threes everyone gradually started to slip away back to their cars and their journeys home.

"I think we should go too," Jeff said to Leah.

"I can't! I can't leave Hannah here!"

"Okay, but maybe we need to go when her Mum gets here."

Leah nodded her head in agreement.

It seemed like they were waiting an age for Mrs Wagstaff to arrive. The blue light of the ambulance still illuminated the dark spring night sky as Mrs Wagstaff entered the leisure centre with a dark-haired man in his late-40s with a blanket wrapped around her shoulders.

Leah walked gingerly up towards Mrs Wagstaff and Leah just patted her on her shoulder and sadly whispered, "I'm sorry."

Jeff shook the man's hand, who they assumed to be Bill and shepherded them towards the office. Jeff knocked the door, slowly pulled down the handle and Mrs Wagstaff and Bill went in.

Jeff whispered, "We'll leave you to it. Anything... Just ask."

Hannah looked up as Jeff pulled the door closed. He and Leah could hear the start of tears as Hannah raced into her Mum's arms for a hug.

Leah turned her head back towards the door. She wanted to help but didn't know how.

Jeff put his arm around Leah's shoulder, "Come on. It's their moment. They need to be alone."

As the sliding door of the leisure centre opened automatically before them, they heard the door of the office opening.

Bill came out of the room and went over to get a drink from the café.

Before Jeff could stop her, Leah dashed over.

"How are they? What happens now?" she spurted out.

Bill took a sip of his coffee.

"They will take Harry back to the hospital shortly, whenever Hannah and Dorothy are ready. I'll stay here until then and take them home."

"Thank you," Leah said politely.

"Did you know him well?" he asked.

"Very," Leah replied. "He is... was..." she said, correcting herself, "My manager... my mentor... my friend."

Leah hadn't cried so far. She did now.

Chapter 13

Leah didn't want to go to school.

Harry was her manager. Her mentor. Her friend. He might as well as been her grandfather, the amount of love and care he showed for her.

She pulled the duvet over her head and was still in her makeshift den when her Mum came in with a cup of tea and a couple of slices of heavily jammed toast.

"Hey! Get this down you. You have to eat," Rose said.

Leah didn't know what to say in response, so she peeped out briefly to see what her Mum had brought her and went back under the duvet.

"I'll phone the school," Rose said quietly. "I'll tell them you have a stomach bug, although I'm sure they'll know the real reason."

"Thanks Mum," the words muffled by the duvet were barely audible.

Leah emerged from the duvet and sat there staring at the wall, her tea almost going cold as she nearly forgot to drink it.

She took small little mouse-like bites from her toast. She didn't have much appetite. It was a trauma no-one should have to go through. To hear Harry had passed away would have been bad enough – to see him lying there was painful. When she closed her eyes, the silhouette of Harry's frame was still imprinted on her mind.

She was at least grateful that she hadn't been the one who had run to see where Harry was, hadn't been the one to discover his collapsed body. How must poor Daisy be feeling?

Rose had turned Leah's phone off overnight and taken it off her. She wanted her to sleep and wanted her not to text her teammates all night.

Leah stumbled out of the sanctuary of her bed and dragged her frame into the kitchen where her Mum was tidying away the breakfast dishes.

"Oh, hi love!"

Leah grunted a response.

"School said hope you feel better over the weekend and get back into school for Monday. There's a few of your team off with stomach bugs today."

Rose handed Leah her phone.

"Here. You had better see if anyone has text you overnight."

Leah's phone sprung into life and a barrage of pings and beeps signified a whole host of texts and voicemail alerts awaiting her attention.

There were eight from her teammates at Marshbrook, a text and a voicemail off Hannah and several unknown numbers which she quickly discovered were from some of the Deadtail Dragons who had changed their phones since she had played there two years ago.

Leah showed the inbox to her Mum.

"Do you want me to?"

Leah nodded.

"Okay. Hannah first."

Rose opened the text that simply said, "Left you a voicemail. Thanks for being there for me last night. X"

Rose played the voicemail on loud speaker. If they hadn't known it was Hannah they would have struggled to recognise her voice. Naturally, there was none of the usual chirpiness in her tone.

"Hi Leah, it's Hannah. Erm… I dunno where to start really. Just… erm… thanks for your support last night. Erm… my Dad thought the world of you. He was the best. Erm… obviously at some point, am going to need to meet up. He'd want you to be happy that you knew him. Not sad that he's… erm… gone. Will text you tomorrow. Trying to get the league to call Sunday's game off. Don't think any of us can play football right now. Even though Dad would have wanted us to. Look after yourself. Love you."

Leah cried.

She'd tried to hold the tears in when she knew there was a voicemail to listen to, but the words 'Dad thought the world of you' was enough to reduce anyone to tears.

The texts from her teammates were much the same.

"Oh my word"

"What a shock!"

"Poor Daisy!"

"Poor Hannah"

"Poor Harry!"

Leah's boyfriend Luke had passed the news onto his old teammates at Deadtail Dragons and the texts they sent were typical of their boyish charm.

"Gutted!"

"Wounded!"

"Legend!"

"Madness!"

They all asked to be kept updated as to when the funeral would be and, like Leah, they saw Harry as a father/grandfather figure and would bunk the day off school to attend his final journey.

Within 24 hours, the league had confirmed with Littleborough that the weekend's game could be delayed until a fortnight later and that Marshbrook's home game scheduled for the following Sunday with Barnstone Belles could also be postponed until after the funeral.

It gave Hannah the opportunity to cancel the Thursday night training session knowing they had no game to prepare for.

Time was never going to be a quick healer but Leah popped round to see Hannah and Dorothy on a couple of occasions.

On one visit to the Wagstaffs, Leah was let into the house by Hannah and they could distinctly hear giggling in the living room where Dorothy was in conversation with the local vicar about the funeral arrangements.

Leah slid onto a stool in the kitchen, adjacent to Hannah who was reaching into the cupboard for something.

Hannah handed Leah a small white envelope with Leah 'Elmshore written neatly on the front.

"What's this?" Leah asked.

"Open it."

Leah slid her finger under the seal of the envelope and carefully opened it. She looked inside and saw what appeared to be a cheque.

"What the –?"

"Dad had a Will. He mentioned you in it. He specifically said the envelope had to be addressed to Leah 'Elmshore too," Hannah chuckled.

"But…"

"But nothing, take it out the envelope."

Leah's slender fingers gripped the edge of the cheque and pulled it from the envelope. The front was facing away from her. She had to turn it round to see what it said.

"A hundred pounds! What the –" Leah exclaimed.

"It's what he wanted you to have. He said in his will that football's an expensive hobby these days and he mentioned when your Dad was out of work that he didn't want to lose you from football just for the sake of a few bob!"

"I'm… er… kinda… speechless," Leah stammered. "Erm… thankyou boss!"

"At least you can pay your brother back for the money he gave you for the boots!"

"Yeah, and I might get some decent ones! I haven't scored any goals since I got the yellow ones!"

Hannah chuckled.

"Good to see a sort of a smile from you," Leah said.

"Have to try!" Hannah replied. "One of Dad's favourite sayings was, 'The world's a better place when you don't hide'."

There was more laughter from the front room.

"I need to investigate what's so funny!" Hannah said, getting up from her stool in the kitchen.

Leah followed as Hannah opened the door to the front room where Dorothy and the vicar were sat at the dining table, overlooking a tablet. Leah was shocked that the vicar had a technological know-how.

The vicar wrote something in his diary and Dorothy put her thumbs up for approval.

"What's going on?" Hannah asked. "I've never heard so much laughter before! Certainly not at a time like this!"

"Oh, sorry Hannah!" Dorothy replied. "We're just doing the Order of Service for the funeral. The way your Dad would have liked it!"

"Dare I ask?" Hannah asked.

"I'll show you later," Dorothy answered.

The vicar spoke calmly. "It's a time for sadness but a time for remembering the good things about Harry too."

"I know. It's just such a shock still," Hannah said sorrowfully.

The vicar opened his Bible. "There's 'a time to be born and a time to die. A time to plant and a time to harvest. A time to kill and a time to heal. A time to tear down and a time to build up'."

Hannah didn't know what to say.

"Sometimes," he continued, "people build up again before they have the time to heal. Everyone's different. Right now," he said, gesticulating toward Dorothy, "your Mum is at the remembering the happy times stage. The time will come where she'll need to grieve and need to heal."

Hannah seemed to understand.

"Did you...?" Dorothy asked.

"Yes," Hannah replied, pointing towards Leah's hand that still held onto the envelope.

"Oh good! It's what he wanted," Dorothy said, smiling in the direction of Leah.

"Erm... thanks. I'm... erm... touched," Leah stammered out.

"Don't thank us!" Dorothy said. "It's **you** we need to thank."

"Why?" Leah asked, confused.

"Harry was all set to quit football with those Deadtail Dragons. You gave him his zest to carry on again."

Hannah put her arm around Leah as a tear rolled down her cheek.

Dorothy continued, "He loved working with you Leah. You made it all worthwhile for him again. He died happy. He died doing what he loved the most."

The vicar stood and smiled at the three ladies. "I'll be in touch sometime tomorrow, Dorothy," he said.

"Thank you. Hannah, show him out will you?"

Hannah walked with the vicar towards the door and Dorothy called Leah over to her.

"Leah," she said, "it would give me great delight, if you are up to it, to stand at the door of the church and hand out the Order of Service booklets. Would you?"

"Erm, yeah, can Luke do it with me?"

"Of course. That was what I had hoped."

Chapter 14

Leah and Luke stood proudly at the door of the church as the well-wishers filed in to pay their final respects to Harry Wagstaff.

Hannah and Dorothy had worked closely with the vicar to produce an Order of Service booklet that was true to Harry's life as a man and life as a football man.

On the front was Harry's picture and the words **We say goodbye to 'Arry Wagstaff** printed in a large, bold font.

Even up to the last minute, Hannah had been undecided whether to put 'Arry or Harry. In the end, it was the vicar that said it wouldn't be right not to feature Harry in the way that people knew him best. A man who never could say his aitches, a man named 'Harry' by his unknowing parents!

The H theme continued throughout the funeral service. His favourite hymn had always been *How Great Thou Art* and when people opened the booklet to sing the opening hymn there were murmurs and chuckles as the lyrics were printed *'Ow Great They Art* and the vicar instructed those present to, "sing as Harry would have sung."

Hymn two was *'Oly 'Oly 'Oly* and the final one was the traditional F.A. Cup Final hymn *Abide with Me* with the opening verse typed out as

> 'Abide with me: fast falls the eventide;
> The darkness deepens; Lord, with me abide:
> When other 'elpers fail and comforts flee,
> 'elp of the 'elpless, O abide with me.'

Even the songwriters were listed with the H missing from Henry!

At the crematorium, the minister in charge of the ceremony, drew the curtains around the coffin.

"Harry was a football man. He was a church man. He had a strong faith. A strong belief to give his football knowledge to those who were prepared to listen. And now, Harry is coming home."

The minister stepped aside and faint music could be heard through the speakers, gradually faded up until everyone could make out the familiar vocal of the England football song *Three Lions* – "It's coming home, It's coming home, It's coming, Football's coming home."

"Harry's coming home!" said Scott Smithson.

"Here, Leah!" Kenny called over.

"Hey!"

"I wanna say something to everyone."

"What do you mean?"

Kenny fumbled in his pocket for a crumpled up piece of paper, a little torn by the house keys and other bits and pieces that were in the pocket with it.

"Here," he said, handing it to Leah.

Leah could hardly make out what he had written, looking like, as many teachers say, a spider had crawled all over the paper!

"What does it say?"

"That he was the best. Saw the best in all of us. I just wanna tell everyone that."

"Come with me."

Leah and Kenny walked over to where the vicar was.

"Erm... excuse me," Leah called out courageously and whispered in the vicar's ear what Kenny wanted to do.

The vicar cleared his throat which grabbed everyone's attention.

"Erm, ladies and gentlemen, this young man would like to say a few words."

Kenny stood up tall, despite being more nervous about it than anything he had ever done in his life.

"Erm... I ain't good with words," he said. "So I wrote it down first. Probably spelt it all wrong mind you."

A couple of his Deadtail teammates sniggered.

"Erm... I erm... just wanted to say that me and the Deadtail lads really are no-hopers. Other than Luke who's gonna make it good and Leah of course."

Hannah clapped briefly.

"Erm... any way... erm... like I said, we would have been causing all sort of trouble if Harry hadn't tried his best to make us into something useful."

A few more people clapped.

"Erm. So, I erm… just wanted to say a saying that Harry told me the very first time I said to him I was rubbish at football."

The whole room stood silently and looked at Kenny, who was still shaking like a leaf.

"Erm, he said, 'Nothing is worthless for the one who sees the gold' and I said I haven't got any gold in me. He said, 'Everyone has, you just have to look for it.' And he was right."

Everyone applauded.

Kenny's twin Scott was crying again, which got his teammates playfully punching him and calling him names!

"So, erm… thanks Harry… Erm… 'Arry… You were a true diamond even if before she came along," as he pointed to Leah, "we couldn't win a game when you was our manager!"

Kenny looked at the vicar, "Was that okay your highness?"

Everyone laughed. Kenny looked blank, then decided he might as well laugh with everyone else.

Dorothy made her way slowly over to Kenny and gave him a huge hug that made him feel uncomfortable. It also gave him a warm glow inside that he hadn't felt too often during his troubled life.

"They were very kind words," she whispered. "Harry would have been so proud of you for standing up to say that."

The congregation smiled through the tears. There wasn't a dry eye in the room. Even the hard, tough players from Deadtail Dragons were crying. As the music faded out, Kenny and Scott Smithson muttered, "Only man who believed in us. Only man who cared."

The funeral had been arranged for a Saturday, so that none of the many youngsters Harry had coached had to miss a day's school.

It also meant that when the ceremony was over, no-one really had anything to do that afternoon other than gather at the local carvery pub where sandwiches were laid on for everyone to gather and have a natter about Harry.

The vicar from the church pinged a wine glass with a fork to try and get everyone's attention, before asking everyone to bow their heads in a last prayer for Harry.

The Deadtail Dragons players all gathered in one corner, as ever, a scruffy looking lot with some of them showing the early signs of growing rather puny beards and moustaches.

As they were when Leah played for them, not many of them had much hair on their head!

The lads chatted away with Leah, who introduced some of them to some of the Marshbrook girls as the afternoon went on.

Some of the Deadtail Dragons boys were looking at the Marshbrook Maidens wondering if they had boyfriends or not, while the Maidens were wondering which of the lads got into the most trouble at school, if they even went in the first place!

Daisy whispered to Leah, "You certainly picked the only decent boy in the team for your boyfriend!"

Leah suppressed a laugh.

Scott and Kenny were having a good natter with Maddy and Zara, which Leah observed involved a lot of laughter, a lot of head shaking, eyes rolling, playful punching and a few glares between them.

She wasn't going to get involved even though curiosity was getting the better of her.

Leah was talking to Hannah when Kenny called her over again.

"Oi, Leah!"

"What?" Leah responded.

"Come here," he shouted, with the other three teenagers beckoning her over too.

"Right!" Kenny said, with great authority.

Leah looked confused.

"Settle an argument..." Kenny said.

"Which is?" she questioned.

"Well, you played footy with us and you played footy with them... Even though Deadtail Dragons were pretty rubbish, are boys better at football than girls?"

"We'd beat you easily!" Zara boasted.

"Whatever!" Scott scoffed.

"Double figures!" said Maddy.

"Enough!" Leah interjected angrily. "We're at a funeral for God's sake!"

"Yeah, sorry," Kenny said sheepishly, looking heavenward to say 'sorry' to Harry too.

Leah looked up too. From somewhere, an idea popped into her head, she assumed from Harry himself.

"Only one way to find out..." Leah said, winking and walking away.

Chapter 15

With no training sessions, and no matches, Leah had acquired two extra nights to sit in the house and two extra weekends with nothing to do.

She had tried to keep herself busy, to take her mind off Harry dying, to take her mind off the funeral, to stop herself from crying.

The first Thursday night after he died, a week to the day, Leah twiddled her thumbs and looked at her football bag knowing why she wasn't going out to train.

Her Dad called her down to watch the football match on the television, hoping to take her mind off it. But, within seconds of the kick off, the co-commentator made some remark about tactics and Leah stormed upstairs muttering, "Harry knows more about football than you ever will!" and sobbed on her bed.

The death of a friend puts a hole in the heart of even the toughest characters and Leah was no different. When she felt the world was against girls playing football, Harry had embraced his new player and helped her achieve her ambitions, albeit with the deception of being called Lee and getting the nickname 'Boy Wonder'!

Then, as Leah had new struggles with waiting and waiting for a chance to play football with her new team, Harry had been the one to help her fly again with his daughter's team the Southsea Swallows. And, had been the lighthouse to guide Leah through the choppy seas back to try again with Marshbrook.

Three years of her footballing life had Harry at the centre, three chapters of her life story.

Eventually, the tears dried up and she turned her thoughts to happier times and fetched out a scrapbook from underneath her bed.

Whenever Deadtail Dragons, Southsea Swallows or Marshbrook Maidens had got a mention in the newspaper (very rare in the case of Deadtail) she cut the article out and stuck it in.

She also scanned it on the printer in her Dad's office and saved it onto the computer. But there was something extra special about keeping a scrapbook of her football career.

Harry had encouraged her to keep it.

"You never know gal, one day you might make it big for England and someone will wanna read the story of Leah 'Elmshore!"

Leah had held onto that dream. The three lions badge on her chest, walking out at Wembley Stadium to represent her country.

In her dream, she always saw her Dad, Mum, Mikey and Harry in the crowd watching her. A dream that could no longer come true in that much detail at least.

"If dreams can't come true," she whispered quietly, talking to Harry in the only team photo of the Deadtail Dragons she had in her book, "what's the point of having them?"

Leah closed the scrapbook, jumped down off the bed and picked up her football bag.

THUD!

She threw it across the room against the opposite wall making an almighty bang.

Before her brother or parents had time to even speak to her, Leah stormed out of the house, "I'm going for a walk. I have my phone!"

Rose and Jeff looked at each other with one of those, 'Leave her to grieve looks' and Rose calmly said, "Okay Leah, don't be too long."

The door closed behind Leah, much more gently this time and Leah walked briskly down the street.

When she reached the crossroads she had a dilemma. Left took her to Luke's but she didn't really want to see him. Right took her towards the Leisure Centre and she certainly didn't want to go there either!

That left straight on which only led to the supermarket, and, checking her pockets, she realised she had enough money for a fizzy drink and a cake so she would go and sit in the café for a while and collect her thoughts.

She sat down as far away from the main part of the store as she could, tucked in the corner of the café near the windows.

She text her Mum to tell her where she was and took a tiny bite from the chocolate éclair she had bought.

She hadn't had much of an appetite over the previous week but she had returned to school after having the one day off.

Leah took a large suck from the red straw in her cup and gulped down the coke before taking another bite from the cake.

Leah started a game of Candy Crush but as soon as she made a wrong move she decided that she really couldn't concentrate on it and swiped the app closed and put her phone back on the table.

She was sat side on to one window and she stared at the traffic going past, quite astonished by the number of people who were driving and on their phones at the same time!

She turned back towards the hustle and bustle of the tills beeping away as people scanned their shopping and wondered whether it was possible to get peace and quiet anywhere!

Her answer was immediate. She was startled to hear a gentle tap turn into a knocking on the window.

If Leah had time to make a top ten of people she didn't want to see right now, the person knocking on the window would be in the top two or three!

Leah mouthed, "Hiya Aunty!" and hoped she wouldn't come bustling in to sit with her.

She did.

"What are you doing here alone? Does your Mum know you are here? Of course she will! You with Luke? Sorry to hear about your manager..." Miriam spurted out in one long breath!

"I... erm... needed time alone," Leah responded, after a pause.

"Oh, er, yes, of course," Miriam stuttered her response. "You, er, know where I am if you want to chat."

Miriam started to shuffle away again.

"You can stay," Leah said, quietly.

"But you said," Miriam replied.

"Yeah, I did need time alone, but it's okay if you stay. You won't talk about football for one thing, and that's the thing right now I don't want to talk about!"

Miriam was about to sit down, but, peering into Leah's cup waddled over to the café till and topped up Leah's drink, returning with that and a pot of tea for herself.

"So, er, **do** you want to talk Leah?"

"Yeah, I guess..."

"It's good news about –" Miriam began, but she couldn't finish what she was about to say.

"Football. Harry," interrupted Leah.

"I thought you said you didn't want to talk about football?"

"I, er... dunno what I want to be truthful, but I don't want to talk about the game itself if that makes sense."

Miriam looked puzzled, "Er, not really."

Leah paused.

"I had a dream to be the best footballer I could be."

Miriam nodded.

Leah continued, "To play at Wembley..."

"You've done that!" Miriam exclaimed, excitedly.

"I suppose so," Leah replied, "but, you know, for England and watching those faces who helped me achieve it look down on me."

"But..."

"But, now what's the point? The person who would have been most proud to see me succeed never will..."

Leah began to cry.

As ever, Miriam was an organised woman and reached into her handbag for a packet of tissues to dry Leah's eyes.

"You thinking of quitting?" Miriam asked.

Leah nodded.

Miriam placed a finger under Leah's chin and lifted her head slowly until Leah was making eye contact with her aunt.

"At church," she said, "we have a group for people to come to when they have lost someone they love. It's not really for a child to attend, but the advice they give works for all ages…"

"Which is?" Leah said, looking sorrowful.

"Don't make any big decisions while you are grieving."

"Huh?" Leah said, confused.

"Your emotions are all over the place. Making decisions right now may end up as the wrong ones. Do you have any matches left this season?"

Leah held up two fingers.

"Get them out of the way, then think about it over the summer break. You owe your old manager and your new manager some loyalty. It's a precious gift, being loyal."

Leah looked up at her aunt.

"Come on, drink up," Miriam ordered. "Do you want a lift home? I could do with seeing your mother anyway."

"Thank you," Leah whispered. "Can I ask you a favour?"

Miriam replied, "Go on."

Leah unfolded the cheque that she had kept in her pocket since she had been given it.

"Will you give this to Mum and ask her to give me the money whenever she can?"

"Of course."

Leah looked out of the car window, increasingly silently on the journey back to her home. Miriam pulled the car onto the drive, Leah whispered a quick, "Thank you" and dashed upstairs to her room. Miriam had Leah's cheque in her hand which she took into the kitchen and gave to Rose.

Leah lay on her bed to text Hannah about the weekend trip to Littleborough and was interrupted by a knock on her bedroom door.

"Yeah?" she answered.

"Hey sport," Jeff said, walking in.

"Hey."

Jeff had his hands behind his back.

"What are you hiding?"

"Left hand or right hand?" Jeff asked, his hands still behind his back.

"Right."

Jeff pulled the right arm from behind his back and lay £90 in ten pound notes on her bed.

"There's the money from the Harry cheque. We will pay it into our account tomorrow. I've given Mikey his £10 back already."

"And the left hand?"

Jeff swung out his left arm which had a piece of paper in it. He handed the printed email to Leah.

Leah read, "Thank you for attending your interview on Wednesday, this is to confirm what we discussed on the phone earlier today. We are delighted to offer you the position, starting on May 14th."

Leah jumped off the bed. "You've got a job!"

"Yup!" Jeff said, positively. "No more scrimping and saving again I hope! You can carry on at football and so can Mikey if he wants to!"

"Yay!"

They hugged.

"Dad," she continued. "Do you believe in good and bad luck?"

"I'm not sure," he said. "Why?"

"Well, since my boots ripped and I got the new ones, I haven't scored since... And I could always keep them as a spare pair if we got some new ones..."

"We're not made of money though, you know?"

Leah pointed at the money on her bed. "There is this," she said.

Jeff waited in the car while Leah went off boot shopping eventually returning to the car with two bags.

"All done?"

"Yup."

"What's in the other one?"

"Nothing that a Dad needs to see!" Leah responded.

The Littleborough match rolled around quickly and Leah felt happy in her new boots at training and gave Maddy a hard time in goal with some vicious shots at goal.

Marshbrook started badly with the lack of training and Littleborough, with a lot of new players from the opening day thrashing, raced into a 2-0 lead.

Natasha Holmes pulled a goal back for the Maidens while Leah tried everything she could do to score. She was desperate. She had never been so keen to score and was frustrated when things weren't going her way. She had even picked up a yellow card from the referee for kicking the ball away with frustration.

She looked up and said, "Come on Harry, I need a goal!"

Eventually, Eloise came forward from defence, sprinted towards the penalty area and slid a sideways pass to Leah.

Come on, Leah thought to herself and swung her right leg back and then forward in perfect timing to connect with the ball.

The ball sped off her boot like a rocket into the roof of the net! 2-2! Leah had scored.

The adrenalin rush was huge inside Leah's head and she ripped off her football top, so fast she almost pulled up the T shirt that was underneath which would have showed the whole world her bra!

Quickly adjusting things again, she ran towards Hannah, her white T-shirt displaying black writing 'That's for you 'Arry!'

Unfortunately for Leah, the referee was a stickler for the rules and walked up to Leah and showed her a second yellow card for removing her shirt in the goal celebration, which was quickly followed by a red card.

Leah couldn't believe it! Surely the referee could ignore the rules on this occasion?

The referee even said, "Sorry, it's the rules!" as she showed it.

It meant that Leah would miss the last game of the season at home to Barnstone Belles, a game Marshbrook won 1-0 with a late Niamh Oliver penalty.

Hannah shook all the players' hands as they left the field of play and sat them all down in a circle round her. "Well, that's that then! Another season over!"

"Erm, not quite," Leah said.

"Oh?" Hannah questioned.

Some of the girls sniggered. They had been in on the secret since a couple of days after Harry's funeral.

Leah explained.

"At Harry's farewell, there was a bit of a 'discussion' between Kenny, Scott, Maddy and Zara," Leah wiggled two fingers to suggest speech marks around the word "discussion" when she really meant an argument.

"Are boys better than girls?" Zara exclaimed.

"Oh," Hannah said, guessing where this was going.

Leah continued, "Yeah, next Saturday for the 'Arry Wagstaff cup, we are playing Deadtail Dragons in a classic Boys versus Girls showdown!"

"Oh my!" Hannah chuckled.

"You're **our** manager," Leah said, looking at Hannah.

"And mine and Leah's Dads," Zara said, "will manage those rough boys!"

Saturday couldn't come round quickly enough and there was a week of banter on Facebook and in texts as to who was going to win.

Thankfully for Luke and Leah, there wasn't going to be a direct boyfriend versus girlfriend match up. As Luke had a schoolboy's contract with his club, it wouldn't allow him to take part in a game that wasn't authorised by them.

Mikey stood next to his Dad, both of them in tracksuits and football boots bellowing out instructions from the dugouts as the game got under way. Zara's Dad became the referee, when they realised they might need one!

The first whistle blew to get the game under way and Marshbrook looked a little nervous, aware that Leah would know that the Deadtail lads would take no prisoners if they thought they were being shown up by some girls!

Leah received the ball though and knew she had the beating of these lads, especially as some of them weren't even playing football any more.

Partly jokingly and partly seriously, Kenny and Scott tried to squish Leah between them as she tried to attack the goal. Two years ago, Leah had made fools of them running past them. This time they were going to win and they knocked Leah flying with a crunching shoulder barge from either side.

"Hey! That's my daughter!" Jeff hollered, forgetting at that moment he was the manager of the lads that had just done it!

Leah dusted herself off and Zara's Dad had awarded a free kick which Leah took quickly, curling an effort just wide of the goal where Adam Vale deputised in Luke's absence.

Damien Bond had bulked out a bit since he was in Year 7 and was actually playing rugby for a local side in his spare time these days.

It meant he had a good awareness of what was going on around him and still had a bit of football skill, firing a powerful shot goalwards and beyond the grasp of Maddy to give Deadtail a 1-0 lead.

Marshbrook weren't finished though and it was no surprise that they levelled the score, with a clever run from Leah that took all the Dragons by surprise. As the remaining defenders ran out to stop her, she back-heeled the ball to an unmarked Natasha Holmes to make it 1-1.

Both sides huffed and puffed but neither were able to find a vital breakthrough to take the lead in the game.

Jeff looked at his watch. Ten minutes to go until the final whistle.

"Sub please!" he called out.

The Deadtail Dragons players looked at Jeff in bewilderment.

"We don't have any!" they called.

Marshbrook looked confused too.

"Kenny, off you come," Jeff called, as the remaining players looked towards Jeff to see what was going on.

Kenny walked slowly towards the touchline, still clueless as to who was coming on to replace him. He shook Jeff's hand and shook Mikey's hand as he came off.

"Who's coming on?" the referee asked.

There was a long pause before a voice said, "Me!"

"YOU!?" said probably everyone except Jeff.

He undid his tracksuit top, pulled down his tracksuit trousers and Mikey walked out onto the pitch.

"Come on Ref!" some of the Marshbrook players complained.

The referee called over Leah and went up to speak to Mikey with her, "Are you sure little bro?" she asked.

"Yup!" he smiled.

"Okay! Play on!" said Zara's Dad.

Before anyone had chance to ask "Is he any good?" Mikey received the ball from Adam Vale's goal kick and calmly and accurately passed it to Damien.

Damien looked up and chipped a pass forward that flew over everyone's heads and a fast-paced Mikey was the first to react, running after it as fast as his little legs would carry him.

He got to the ball first and managed to get the ball under control.

Every pair of eyes was on him, surely Mikey couldn't shoot as well as control the ball?

Mikey swung back a clumsy foot and was about to connect with the ball with his toes rather than the instep of his boot.

"No you don't!" Leah said, having sneaked up behind him, grabbing her younger brother round his chest and pulling him back.

"Penalty!" declared the referee.

"What?!" screamed Leah, pointing to where the holding had taken place.

"Good point!" said Zara's Dad.

"Phew!" said Leah.

"Anyway, it's full-time!" he declared and blew the final whistle.

"What now?" Hannah and Jeff asked. "We hadn't anticipated a draw," Hannah continued.

"No! We thought we'd win easily!" said Jeff.

"Likewise!" said Hannah.

Leah smiled, "To use a word 'Arry would say, let's call this an 'onourable draw!"

Also available

Leah and the Football Dragons

There are all kinds of dragons. There are successful dragons who always win and sit on their piles of gold. And then there are the Deadtail Dragons, a boys' football team who know only of defeat.

There is only one talented footballer who can change the fortunes of the Deadtail Dragons. And there is just one problem. That footballer is a girl.

How can Leah win when her local football teams only accept boys? How can she succeed when they tell her that 'Girls can't play football'?

Taking her own destiny in her hands Leah comes up with a bold plan to both fulfil her sporting dreams and help the Deadtail Dragons to fly.

Leah and the Football Dragons is a story for children aged 8 upwards.

www.paulmullinsauthor.co.uk

Also available

Leah and the Waiting Game

For Leah, life is about to become a waiting game.

After dragons have been defeated it is not always happily ever after. There are new adventures to be had. And in the meantime, there is waiting...

...Waiting to hear the news that she longs to hear.

...Waiting for all kinds of results.

...Waiting to make new goals.

What can Leah do while she is waiting? She can only do what she is good at. She can do what she loves. She can play football.

But as she struggles to find her place in her world, she encounters a whole new set of challenges.

Challenges that could overwhelm even a modern-day teenager like Leah.

www.paulmullinsauthor.co.uk

55759965R00063

Made in the USA
Charleston, SC
08 May 2016